THE ALLIANCE OF HEROES

FINISH THE TEACHERS FISRT

A NOVEL

HAJI RAZMI

ISBN
978-1-964804-91-0 (Paperback)
978-1-964804-90-3 (eBook)
978-1-964804-92-7 (Hardcover)

The Alliance of Heeroes

Haji Razmi

Table of Contents

Chapter 1

Chairman Murad Khan

"I am known in the whole world, from here to London, from Pakistan to America, I am known everywhere as the hero of Jihad! I don't like anarchy in my family, no one is free to do everything they want without my permission. When I say no to anything, that thing cannot be done even if it costs my life. You all know me very well. I am the boss here, nobody can disobey me. Tell this rude boy not to mess up with me or I will throw him out of my house for good!"

Chairman Murad Khan threw his hands in the air and spoke as thunderous as possible. "I will never allow him to marry the daughter of this bastard, the daughter of this Russian puppet. Does my stupid son have any idea that this son of a bitch murdered my brother? Had it not been for the Americans here, I would have cut his bones into pieces. You know? I myself sent dozens of dogs like him to hell in the times of Jihad!"

He took a deep breath and loosened his tie.

"Nowadays, there are ridiculous things going on in this country. They call it the time of national reconciliation, the time of democracy, and because there are Americans in the country, every murderer can walk free. If it were not for these stupid things, I would have beheaded his infants in the cradle; I am still thirsty for this son of a bitch's blood."

Chairman Murad Khan took a Herati handkerchief out of his slacks' pocket and held it to his mouth to prevent the spill of his saliva, caused by a severe cough, lasting a good few seconds.

His senior wife rushed to the kitchen and quickly returned with a glass of water. She put the glass of water into her husband's hand. "Drink some water *Wolaswal Sahib* for God's sake, don't agonize yourself, God forbid you will be suffering."

Chairman Murad Khan stared at his senior wife, pushing her hand along with the glass of water away from him. He took another deep breath.

"Call him *rayes sahib*! He is now the chairman of the provincial council. You stupid don't know that yet?" Khan's middle wife whispered in Dordana's ear.

"I am sorry *rayes sahib,* it was my mistake, sometimes my memory doesn't work well," said Dordana. "Please drink the water."

Some years ago, Murad Khan had served as the *wolaswal-* the district governor of Andkhoy, a northwestern district in the province of Faryab. Therefore, per his own order that he expressed to his family, he should be called *Wolaswal Sahib*-Mister District Governor by every member of his family for the rest of his life, unless he were appointed to a higher government position with a more exalted title. Three months ago he had been "elected" as the *rayes* or chairman of the provincial council of Faryab; hence he must be now called *rayes* sahib- Mister Chairman.

He held the handkerchief to his mouth a few more seconds, and then grabbed the glass of water from Dordana, who was still holding the glass out to him. He took a sip of the water.

"Nowadays the times are so brazen that one's children don't listen to their father, they do whatever they wish." He looked around to make sure all 25 people present in the family meeting were paying adequate attention to his speech. "In my family, no one can get married without my permission, you cannot bring any dog and cat into my family!" He lit a cigarette and puffed dark smoke into the air. "This is our tradition; this is what our fathers and forefathers have done. Fathers select the life mates of their sons and daughters!"

A long silence filled the room, broken only by Khan's coughing.

"I know it was my fault that I brought this stupid boy to the capital," he said remorsefully. "Here he learned extreme rudeness; you all heard him how vulgarly and shamelessly he said to me that he didn't need me anymore, that now he can earn his own living."

Khan extended his left hand toward the ashtray in front of him, crushing the half smoked cigarette in it. Then he turned to his senior son.

"What were that shit he said, *hoqoqe bashar*, and *hoqoqe madani*? What garble was that he talked about?"

Khan's senior son threw his hand in the air. "Don't bother *rayes sahib* about his stupid words, whatever he said was garbage. I can take care of him, if you give me your permission, I will punish him so harshly that he will never in his life say such things to you again."

Khan nodded with deep satisfaction to his senior son and tried to say something, but a severe cough prevented him.

All the adults present in the big family hall of the house showed their sympathy toward the head of their family by offering their prayers. His senior wife Dordana and middle wife Latifa were competing in comforting their husband.

Doradana was in her upper sixties. She was known among friends and family as the ill-fated wife of the Khan because she had never given birth to a son. She had four daughters, now all married with children. She was, therefore, trying extremely hard to compete with Khan's other wives in serving him fast.

"For God's sake *rayes sahib*, don't stress up yourself. God punish whoever gives you trouble when you are uncomfortable, I feel deep in my heart for you." Her voice was humble.

Latifa, Khan's second wife, had just turned 45 last month. On top of three obedient daughters, she had brought to the world two well-trained sons. She did not allow being behind in the competition of serving her husband. She pulled herself closer to him, held his left hand in her right and whispered to him in a comforting voice:

"You don't worry *rayes sahib*, may God give you good health, and punish anyone whoever doesn't listen to you. God gave you two such strong sons like Azam and Akram; they will obey you all the time." Latifa pointed to her two sons, sitting next to their father and looking ready to do anything for him, including punishing Samim.

Samim, the renegade son of Khan's younger wife had left today's family gathering after accusing his father of not being respectful of *hoqoqe basher* and *hoqoqe madani*-human rights and civil rights.

Khan's younger wife, Sheren, and her three daughters, ages 16, 14 and 9, were groaning internally, not daring to utter a word.

. They were trying to make themselves busy with cleaning up the house, cooking and preparing lunch. Sheren was worried about Samim, who left the house in protest of his father's stand on his personal issue of getting married to a girl of his choice. She moved back and forth between the family room and the kitchen, trying to listen to what was being said about her son.

"Look, Sheren," shouted Khan as Sheren returned to the family room. "I warned you several times to open your son's eyes, tell him not to go after this daughter of a dog, but I still hear he did not stop seeing her. Why?"

"I told you, *rayes sahib*, he said he was not going after that girl anymore."

"Shut up, he is a liar. I know he still is." Khan removed his fur hat and put it on the pillow next to him. "Do you think I am blind? Do you think when I am not here I don't see what's going on here? I have people following him anywhere he goes. I have people patrolling around this house day and night." Khan lit up another cigarette and coughed a couple of times. "I built this million dollar house for you and your children; I made you and your children equal to the dignitaries of the capital. But your son is now trying to play with my dignity; he is trying to ruin my reputation and bring shame on me, he is trying to become the son-in-law of my enemy. I will never allow this to happen. If he doesn't stop what he is trying to do, I swear to God I will either finish him or finish the father of that prostitute girl!"

Sheren knew her husband very well; she knew that when he was mad at anyone-no matter whom, he would punish that person to the point of death.

Khan noticed that Sheren and her daughters were not paying full attention to what he was angry about, he shouted furiously: "Why are you getting away from me? Come here, all of you! Sit down and stop doing anything while I am talking! For the last time let Samim know, if he doesn't stop seeing this daughter of a pig, I am going to bar him from coming to my house. I will no longer consider him my son!" He blew dark smoke into the air and pointed his finger at Sheren. "You pack up today; I want to take you all back to Andkhoy because you don't deserve living in this house anymore."

Tears shone in Sheren's eyes. "What about our daughters, *rayes sahib*, they are going to school here, there is no girls' high school there."

"I don't care about their school anymore, I cannot leave them here; they will be rude to me too, in the future."

Sheren had always tried to make her children dearer to their father, and for achieving this goal she would try to make him happy by obeying him and supporting him before their children. But now that the future of her children was in danger, she could not stay silent.

"For God's sake, *rayes sahib*, what did the girls do wrong, why do you punish them? Also, Samim is now a grown up boy, he knows right from wrong, be a little patient with him. He is today's young man, we should be talking to him in a nicer way." Sheren numbly wiped her tears with her pink veil.

Khan stared at her with his eyes flashing and his lips quivering:

"Did you all hear that?" He looked around the room. "Why should I blame my son who has come out of such a stupid mother's belly? If you utter another word like that, I will smash your bones, you jenny!" He kept his eyes locked on Sheren.

Today's family meeting was attended by his all three wives, his sons and daughters and their spouses, his brother and sister and their spouses as well as his grandchildren, most of whom were teens. He'd brought Dordana and Latifa and their daughters from Faryab in his new Hummer, and summoned other family members who were living in and around Kabul to this meeting in order to teach his son Samim a lesson about the issue of marriage, and in the meantime, to make his other single children and grandchildren aware of his rules in this regard.

He looked tired and sleepless. His beard and mustache sprouted wildly, gray strands showing in them; due to the stress caused by Samim's non-obedience, he had not had the patience to trim and color them for weeks. Khan was a person with style, whenever he went to meetings with dignitaries; he would dress up in a three-piece suit, a white shirt, and a red tie. He also liked to wear a fancy *Qara Qul-* fur hat. Today also, he had put on his favorite gray suit, white shirt and red tie, because he thought he should appear before his large family as a chairman, as a dignitary, and as a modern-looking man in order to impress his family, especially his educated son Samim, whom he thought was unfairly thinking of him as an uneducated and uncivilized person.

Murad Khan was not used to being confronted in front of his family, especially by one of his wives. His face reddened and his hands were trembling at the argument made by his younger wife.

"Now what!" he cried. "For God's sake, my wife Sheren is now arguing with me. You all know that it was me who brought this woman to Kabul, here I built a palace for her, and here she is enjoying having electricity and running water, that's exactly why she is now disrespecting me." He tried to lower his voice to conceal his chest congestion and wheezing causing cracks in his voice. "Did you forget that on the first night of our wedding you promised me that you would never argue with me? Don't think that now I am an old and weak man! You know I have a thousand armed soldiers under my command. Now I have more power here and there." He pointed at his other sons indicating that they would do anything for him that he wishes. His two sons, sitting next to him nodded in confirmation of their father as they were delighted to see him mad at Samim, who had been receiving the most favorable attention from their father, and whose mother had been favored over theirs all along.

"I did not say anything bad, *rayes sahib,* may God cut out my tongue if I had said anything rude to you," cried Sheren, running toward Khan and bending toward his hands for kissing.

"Get away from me." He pushed her hard enough that her bottom hit the floor.

"You both are *Namakharam,* you don't appreciate all the things that I have done for you and your ill-trained son. I brought you to Kabul because I thought he could be a good son for me, I thought after finishing high school, I would buy him a good business here or make him a high ranking government official, that I would make him a successful and rich man. I was thinking about finding him a girl from a reputable family like the family of a merchant, like the family of an army general, or even like the family of a cabinet member."

He was silent for a moment, staring at the ceiling as if he were trying to remember other things that he had in mind for his son. "You are aware that I have been giving him plenty of money for his daily expenses, and you know he was such a senseless extravagant in comparison to my other children, spending money like sand."

Khan took a deep breath, got up with his hands pressed on his knees, took his fur hat with him, and gestured to Latifa to get his coat and follow him to the second floor. Before laying his foot on the first step toward the second floor, he stopped and signaled to Azam and Akram by a slight nod. They ran toward him, listened attentively to orders that he whispered in their ears. Then Khan walked upstairs, and the two police officers said goodbye to everyone and left the house.

For the past couple of years, Khan had been entertaining his mind with the idea of nominating himself to become a member of the nation's parliament in the upcoming election. He had built this two-story luxury house so that he could be in Kabul frequently and could sometimes invite business leaders, government officials, parliament members, army generals and so on to make friend with them. It had cost him over a million dollars to build. On the top floor, there was a huge master bedroom with a sliding door opening out to a covered balcony, a master bathroom with shower tub, Jacuzzi and walk-in closet, a living room furnished with three burgundy leather couches, a coffee table with a beige marble top and a massage chair. On the ground floor, there were five bedrooms, a family room, and a huge guest room with a separate bathroom, as well as a gigantic modern kitchen.

Khan had hired a Chinese construction company to build this house and had imported high-quality materials such as marble backsplash tile, wood flooring, and wood tile for the roof, high-quality cherry cabinets and doors from China. Also, he had ordered furniture from Germany and brought hand-made rugs from his hometown of Maimana.

By building this house, Khan tried to kill two birds with one stone: to make his younger wife Sheren happy, and to please his VIP guests by inviting them to a luxurious, clean and well-organized house. He would serve his guests wonderful and delicious foods, hand cooked by Sheren, who was known for her culinary delicacies. She had learned cookery from her mother who had lived in Tehran and Kabul for some years. Khan's friends as well as the rest of his family admired Sheren for her cooking skills. Every one of would call her "a sweet-handed lady."

Once in Kabul, Murad Khan liked sometimes to sit in the top floor living room or the balcony alone with Sheren, in seclusion, away from others.

But today, he went out to the balcony, holding Latifa's left hand in his right. They sat down in the corner of the balcony, side by side, each taking a garden chair around a heavy glass table.

Mohammad Murad– Murad for short– was 63 years old. He was born in the city of Maimana, the capital of a northwestern province of Faryab. His father was a smith in one of the disadvantaged areas of the city. Murad had attended a local elementary school but dropped out before finishing his sixth grade.

At the age of thirteen, he and a fellow dropout classmate climbed the wall of one of their neighbors' houses and stole a couple of chickens. They were arrested while trying to sell the chickens to a grocery shopkeeper in another part of the city, who suspected the fowl were stolen and called the police. Murad's friend was let go by the head of the police station just an hour after they were brought in. He later learned that his friend's father had come to the station and paid 200 Afghanis to the chief. Murad, meanwhile, stayed in custody.

The room had mud walls, a small window in the back wall and a shabby carpet on the floor. A security guard with a rubber lash in his hand stood guard in front of the door.

Murad was still a child, and by law, he was not supposed to be put in jail, so they sent for his father to come and pick him up.

Before his father arrived, a middle-aged police officer came into his room, closed the door behind him and ordered Murad to stand up; he stood up. The officer ordered him to get closer to him. He obeyed.

"I am the chief of the police station here and want to warn you that you are a criminal, and we are going to send you to jail," he said. "Maybe you will have to spend two to three months there."

Murad's face went pale, tears appeared in his eyes, and his lips started quivering.

"Don't cry. I can help you, maybe. Maybe I will send you home with your father when he comes today." The officer rubbed his palm over Murad's young, rosy and soft cheeks.

A flash of relief appeared on Murad's face. He clasped the officer's hand in both of his hands and kissed it.

"Do you know, if it were somebody else in my place, he would have beaten you at least a hundred lashes?" The officer spoke in an intimate tone, putting his left arm around Murad's shoulder and pulling him a bit closer.

Murad couldn't tell if the officer's approach towards his body was fatherly or something else. But when the officer's hand slithered down toward Murad's bottom, he pulled away himself from the officer's hand and started crying.

"Why are you crying, you son of a bitch?" shouted the officer. "I am trying to help you; I have children older than you. If you say anything bad about me, I am going to ruin your life, okay?" The chief of police left the room, slamming the door.

Young Murad felt a twist in his stomach. "He is a big person in the government; he is my father's age, why did he try to do b*achabazy* on me? Doesn't he have a wife?"

His thoughts were interrupted by a noise just outside of the detention room. He listened carefully, and as he moved closer to the door, he was pushed backward violently by the opening door and hit the ground. A policeman was pulling a young man in his twenties into the room while kicking and punching him repeatedly. Once both men were inside, the chief rushed into the room too.

"Beat this son of a bitch as hard as you can," the chief ordered his policeman, kicking the man hard in the back several times. "Don't let this son of a donkey go until he confesses."

"For God's sake, what is my fault? What sin did I commit that you are beating me for?" cried the man, tossing and turning on the floor and trying to protect his face from the strikes of the rubber whip by covering it with both of his hands.

"You committed a big crime," replied the policeman, panting. "You stole a coat from that store, worth 150 Afghanis." The policeman struck the suspect's back with the lash.

"I swear to God I did not, the other guy who ran away, did it. I was there just looking."

"No, you son of a bitch, you did it. You were with him."

Murad watched the scene with bewilderment. His body was shaking. He thought, "If you are a policeman, you have the power to arrest people, to beat them and to put them in jail. When I become a policeman, I can arrest and beat the shopkeeper who called the police on you."

There was a kick at the door, and the chief officer entered as hasty as a cat chasing a mouse.

"Is this son of a bitch confessing to the shoplifting or not?"

"No sir, he is not."

"For God's sake *Sarmamoor* sahib, I did not steal anything. I swear to God, I swear to the prophet, Mohammad, I did not do it, I did not take out anything with me," cried the suspect, rubbing his left leg which was just brutally kicked on by the chief.

"You son of a bitch, if you don't confess, I am going to cut your fingers with a knife," he warned. "I will not let you go until you confess," he said, looking at and hinting somehow to the policeman to go on beating the man and then marched toward the door.

"For God's sake *Sarmamoor* sahib," shouted the man desperately.

"*Sarmamoor* sahib is very mad at you, you have to please him," the policeman murmured in the man's ears and raised his hand to bring down another blow on the man's legs, but eased his hand, waiting to see what the man was going to say.

"All I have is this watch," said the man, touching with his right hand the old cheap watch on his left wrist.

"What is this shit?" shouted the policeman.

"I swear to God this is all I have."

"Oh, no, do you think *Sarmamoor* sahib is hungry for your junk watch? The policeman brought down the rubber lash on the man's back. "How much money do you have?"

"I have only sixty Afghanis at home, that's all I have."

The policeman paused, pulled back his lash, and ran out in a hurry, closing the door behind him.

In the absence of the policeman, the man indulged himself in putting in his mouth n*aswar-* a mixture of minced tobacco and limestone with intoxicating effect, enjoying a moment of leisure and relief.

"Why are you here?" The man asked Murad.

Murad put his head down and remained silent.

"I know they brought you too in here for money," whispered the man. "These people are very cruel; I swear to God, I didn't steal anything."

"What did the policeman say to you?" asked Murad.

"He said how much money I had? I have only sixty that I made working one week." The conversation of the two inmates was interrupted when the policeman returned in hurry.

"*Sarmamoor* sahib said 200 Afghanis will release you," whispered the policeman, bringing his mouth closer to the man's right ear.

"I swear to Prophet Mohammad I don't have 200," said the man.

"Ok, get up. I go with you, to your home, you give me whatever you have."

The man nodded.

If you are the police, you can beat other people, but no one can beat you. You can get the money from other people, but you don't have to give money to other people. That's because they are police. One time my father said that the belt around police's waist is considered as the belt of the BA BA, King Zahir Shah. Nobody can challenge the power of the King, so never disobey the order of a policeman, it is considered a sin, and your life will be in jeopardy if you disobey them anytime, your life will be tormented both today and on the day of resurrection, Murad was reminding himself.

When Murad's father arrived at the police station, he went straight to the office of the station chief bowing down and trying to kiss his hands.

"*Sarmamoor* sahib, I will be very much grateful to you if you would pardon my boy this time, I promise he will never do this again."

"He deserves to be punished," said the chief, letting Murad's father kiss his hands.

"Wait out there for a minute; I am busy now," he added, hinting something to the policeman in their common sign language.

"Come out with me," the policeman instructed Murad's father, grabbing his arm and pulling him out of the office. "*Sarmamoor* sahib is very upset with you because you are not guiding your son the right way."

"What should have I done? I have been trying all the time to make him a good boy, but he has bad friends, I will try to separate him from them, I swear. But I beg you to do something this time, please tell *Sarmamoor sahib*."

"I will tell him, but you should do something."

"Take this." Murad's father extended his hand toward the policeman with three bills of twenty Afghanis in it.

"This is nothing; he never accepts sixty Afghanis. It's a disgrace to him." The policeman pressed the money back into Murad's father's hand.

Murad's father searched his vest's pockets and came up with two more twenty Afghanis bills.

"That's all I have, I swear to God, I have no more."

The policeman ran to his boss's office as he heard him calling him.

"*Sarmamoor sahib* said I will do you a favor this time for the sake of God but make sure your son never does such a thing again," whispered the policeman as he came back and snatched the hundred Afghanis from Murad's father's hand.

"Go get your son; don't let him do this again."

"Okay, thank you, and God bless you," said Murad's father, running to the officer's office.

"Thank you very much *Sarmamoor sahib*, May God bless you and give you higher positions." He held both his hands over his chest in a show of high respect and gratitude. He then went to the room where his son was locked in.

Murad's head was down; he couldn't get up. He wished the earth would crack and swallowed him rather than facing his father

"Get up, go with your father," shouted the policeman dragging the boy toward the exit door and handing him over to his father.

"Why did you do this, you son of a jenny?" screamed Murad's father, slapping him on the face as soon as they got out of the police station.

"It was not me, the other boy did it," groaned Murad, covering his face with his arms.

"Shut up, you liar! Was it for this that I brought you into this world? You brought shame on me; you ruined my reputation!"

When they got home, Murad's father threw his son in the front room and closed the door behind.

"You gave me a bad name in the whole town, you son of a jenny, today I am going to teach you a lesson that you will never forget in your whole life!"

Murad's father, in his mid40s, was a tall and strong-shouldered man. His job made his arms as stiff as the handle of the heavy hammer that he was using in his smithy shops. He was slapping and punching his son as hard as though forging a thick piece of iron, which not been heated enough in the furnace.

Even though Murad was immensely trying to keep his noise down so that his three little siblings and his mother wouldn't worry about him, but he couldn't help screaming and crying piercingly under the heavy blows on his face, and his head constantly brought by his father. He could hear his mother and his two little brothers and a little sister crying out loud, which was hurting him emotionally. After Murad's father got exhausted of beating Murad, he opened the door and got out of the room.

"It's all your fault, you jenny. I told you so many times to talk to your son, not to let him mingle with those sons of bitches on the street." He shouted at his wife who was standing by the door along with their three kids.

"What's my fault? I have told him that many times, but you are beating him all the times," groaned Murad's mother, entering the room and trying to wipe the dust off Murad's clothes and drying up his tears with her veil.

"Shut up, you jenny, *farsiwan*. He is your son, he is like you, and he will never be of any good to me."

"My mother is not a jenny," cried Murad, trying to stand up on his feet.

"Yes, she is, you don't know, that's why you are so stupid. Shut up!"

After that day, Murad tended to be quiet; he became more and more isolated. His father would no longer take him to the downtown market for Friday grocery shopping. He never traveled alone either ever since as he felt ashamed at the thought of being seen by the person who had called the police on him. He was also ashamed of the neighboring shopkeepers who witnessed him when he got arrested. He even tried to avoid his friends by staying at home days and nights.

He was 15 years old when his mother died of tuberculosis. Within six months of his mother's death, his father married a 16-year-old girl, the daughter of a neighbor, a poor janitor who did not ask for large dowry and did not even ask for a formal wedding ceremony for his daughter. He accepted a lump sum of two thousand Afghanis in return for his daughter.

"Whenever your mother is replaced by a stepmother, your father gets to change into a step farther." He would repeatedly remember this proverb as he witnessed the increasingly hostile attitude of his father towards him and his siblings.

In the past, his father would take Murad with him to the downtown bazaar for the weekly grocery shopping. During the forty minute walk, they would have chats and talks about work and some other stuff. But now, his father did the grocery shopping by himself and left Murad at home. Murad was deeply affected by the change of his father's attitude but had no courage to talk to him about it.

Murad was a hard working young boy, even at the age of 13 and 14, he would volunteer to work closer to the furnace at his father's shop for melting and reshaping hard metals. Some neighboring shopkeepers would tell Murad's father that he had a good son and a good helping hand. But after that incident, Murad was never allowed by his father to collect the money from the customers or touch the cash register. He did receive five Afghanis a week for his seven- days a week hard work. After his mother died, he would spend most of his money buying gum, candy or toys for his three siblings, and keep some money for himself. The other children at home were not receiving cash at all except for the occasion of *Eid*- the religious and national 3-day holidays, which happened twice a year.

As Murad was growing up, his position at home was becoming more formidable. Even though he was rarely subject to his father's beating, but was deeply feeling the callous and uncaring attitude of both his parents. He was becoming, in the meantime more and more sensitive about the way his stepmother was treating his brothers and sister. He would come to their defense more aggressively whenever the stepmother was abusive to them. This caused her to grow more antagonistic towards him. She would try to turn his father against him, even urge him to kick him out of the house. His father was listening to her; they both would try to avoid him as much as possible, not talking to him and even trying to isolate him from his brothers and sister. In the face of all this, they were unable to kick Murad out of their house, but they did succeed in making his life miserable.

Murad finally decided to run away from home forever. He had saved enough money to buy a bus ticket from Maimana to Andkhoy, one of the remote districts of the Faryab province where his uncle and his grandmother lived. When he arrived in Ankhoy bus station, it was easy to find his uncle Sakhidad's teahouse because almost everyone in the small town knew that place. As soon as Sakhidad saw his nephew, he asked him: "Did your father kick you out? I knew it; I knew he would kick you out someday."

Murad extended both of his hands toward his uncles' and kissed them, trying to hide tears in his eyes.

Sakhidad was 45 but the gray color of his beard and mustache made him look older than his age. He was two times widowed, had four daughters from both marriages, three of them already married with children, now living in different parts of the province. His youngest child was a 13-year-old girl, still living with him and his mother. He had owned this teahouse for 20 years, and sometimes he would call the business "his life."

"You know son," said Sakhidad, combing his beard with the fingers of his left hand. "May God bless your mother and May God grant her stay in heaven, she suffered a lot from your father. She had told me several times that he was beating her and you all the times, right?"

Murad nodded.

Sakhidad was doing a good business. In his teahouse, he served *Chainaki*– a traditional Afghan lamb soup, cooked in a ceramic teapot by a charcoal fire. The fresh lamb soup came with turnips, dried sour plums, curry powder and other aromatic spices, and was poured on pieces of freshly baked bread and eaten with the hands. It attracted customers from all around the town.

The place also had a large room, furnished with woolen mattresses and pillows, used during the day as the dining room and by night it was used as a guest room for travelers.

"Son," said Sakhidad to his nephew, "You will be working with me. I am going to let one of the boys go and keep the other one, Ghulam, who is a good hard-working boy. I expect you to be the same. Your job is to wash customers' hands before and after the meals and serve them food and tea, cleaning the room after the travelers leave in the morning, and to replace the water in both hookahs daily. And look, son," Sakhidad got a bit serious, "after cleaning and refreshing the hookahs' water, take that beige colored hookah to the patio, in the back of the teahouse, and that is the only time you can go to the patio, ok?"

"Yes, uncle,"

"Yeah, never ever go out there when people are smoking outside," Sakhidad emphasized.

Murad asked no question, simply nodded with a big smile to show his happiness at being hired so quickly.

"Don't mess with my daughter, ok?" Sakhidad instructed Murad one night when they were walking home after work. "You know, she is a motherless kid, and is very dear to me."

"Uncle, she is like my sister, I will take care of her," Murad assured him.

"I am also letting you know that there is every kind of people coming to my teahouse. There are good people and bad people among them; mullahs, thieves, criminals, smugglers and *bacha baz* people, all kinds of people are my customers. You don't mess with them, just do your job, and if anybody tries to bother you, you let me know."

Murad was listening attentively but wondered why his uncle mentioned *bachabaz* people. He said to himself that he was very well aware of the fact that *bachabazi-* the sexual exploitation of young boys, was commonplace here and everywhere, and that no one can bother him because he was now a grown up guy.

Murad felt safe and happy in his uncle's busyness. He was especially happy when walking together with his uncle between home and work, and was also comfortable at home with his grandmother. His grandmother was delighted seeing her deceased and ill-fated daughter's son living with her, she was very kind to him.

"My grandson deserves a lot of care and kindness, he and his mother suffered a lot from his father," The old lady said to Sakhidad the first night Murad went to their house.

But Murad soon realized that he was not immune from the inconvenience of living with a disciplined employer and uncle on one hand and coping with the attraction of his mischievous, young and pretty daughter on the other. Murad himself was a handsome, tall and well-behaved young man; he had a straight nose and bright eyes. He was shy and polite with the girls, but extremely jealous seeing his cousin playing with the boys next door.

Murad worked in the teahouse from 6 AM to 8 PM, seven days a week. He worked hard and tried to compete with Ghulam, the other worker, whom Sakhidad said was the son of the *chaukidar-* a privately-hired night guard at the bazaar where his teahouse was located.

Ghulam was a couple of years older than Murad and seemed dearer to Sakhidad because he acted like the lead employee whenever Sakhidad was out for daily shopping or other private matter. Ghulam was allowed to do the money part of the job in the absence of Sakhidad as well.

"Your uncle is a very good man," Ghulam told Murad one day around three months after his arrival. "To me, he is like my father."

"Yes, to me too, he is like my father. My mother loved him too."

"What about your own father, do you like him?" asked Murad.

"My father died a long time ago," Ghulam answered.

"Isn't the *chaukidar* your father? My uncle said you are his son?"

"No. He is my uncle and my stepfather. He married my mother after my father died. What about your father, do you like your father?" Ghulam asked his coworker.

Murad paused a bit. "He was good to me sometimes, but he was not good to my mother. He doesn't like my uncle and my grandmother either."

"Why?"

"I don't know." Murad tried to remember something about his parents' relationship.

"When my mother was alive, my father would beat her all the times, and used nasty words to her. Every time when he was mad at my mother, he would call her a jenny *farsiwasn.*"

"What? *Farsiwan?*" Ghulam asked.

"Yes, what is that?"

"Maybe your father is *augho*, is he?"

"I don't know, what is *augho*?" Murad stared at his coworker with extreme curiosity.

"They say *augho* people speak another language. And some people say they are no-good people."

"No, that's not true, my father is a good man."

"But you say he was beating your mother?"

"Yes." Murad felt offended by Ghulam's questions. He was learning that there was a big disparity between his parents' tribal identities. He began questioning himself as to why his parents were fighting all the time, why his father, who was known as a good person in the neighborhood, was not a good husband to his mother. He remembered that his father was an honest man; he never lied, he had told him too never to lie. He never cheated people out of money in his busyness of the smithy shop. Everyone in the neighborhood respected him but why was he like an enemy to his own wife?

Murad was also confused by the fact that all other women in the neighborhood liked his mother. She was a very kind mother; she never cheated on her husband. She was cleaning the house every day, cooking good food, taking care of her children and never used harsh words to them, but still, hated by her husband.

After a week or so, he decided to take this question to her grandmother, as he became frustrated thinking about it.

"Ana!" He called her by the traditional nickname.

"Yes, son."

"Are you *farsiwan* or *augho*?"

The 70-year-old grandma stared at her grandson with astonishment.

"I am *farsiwan*, not *augho*. Why did you ask me that?"

"Baba was calling my mother farsiwan every time he was mad at her. Why?"

The old lady paused, as the signs of annoyance caused further wrinkles in her faded cheeks.

"Son, this is a long story."

"I want to know grandma, what are these things?"

She paused again, fixed her black veil, covering her shoulders and arms with it.

"Your father is a*ugho*."

"What is *augho*?"

"*Augho* people speak *Augho* language, Pashto language."

"No, grandma. He is speaking the same language like you and me."

"Yes, I know. But his father and grandfather spoke that language."

Murad was trying to make sense of the reason that his father was being called *augho* while he was speaking the same language like him, his grandma and his uncle who were not *augho*.

"What is *farsiwan*?" Murad asked.

"We speak Farsi; our tongue is Farsi, that's why they call us *farsiwan*."

"Let's eat dinner," interrupted Sakhidad, who had just entered the room.

"He is asking me questions about *farsiwan* and *augho,*" said the old lady, pointing to Murad.

"You still don't know these things you stupid?" Sakhidad shouted at Murad.

"He is still a child, he doesn't know these things," grandmother said.

"No, he is not a child anymore. He is a grown man, he should know these things," Sakhidad said. "*augho* people were brought to our area from other parts of the country by King Amir Abdul Rahman, long time ago, like 80 or 90 years ago. He brought them here to live here. He gave them our lands, and they made homes here. Sometimes there was fighting between them and our people, Uzbeks. We are true Uzbeks."

"So, they are not good people?" asked Murad.

"What to say, son?" Sakhidad paused, tried to find an appropriate answer to Murad's question. "Maybe there are some good *aughos*, but your father? You know him very well."

Murad was further puzzled by his uncle's explanation, creating more questions than answers in his mind.

"What am I, *farsiwan*, or *augho*?" he asked himself. "My father is *augho*; my mother was *farsiwan*. Am I a good person or bad person? If I follow my father's tribe, I am *augho* and a bad person. If I follow my mother's tribe, then I am a *farsiwan*, the son of a jenny *farsiwan*, as my father called her."

Murad could not sleep well that night and several nights after that as he was trying to determine his real identity.

"How come my mother married my father if he was not a good man?" Murad asked his grandmother one night after his uncle had gone to his bedroom.

"Oh son, you don't know, women cannot say which man to marry and which man not to marry?"

"So why did you and my grandfather- your husband gave your daughter to my father?"

"Son, your mother was given to your father when she was just eight years old, and your father was 11. They were small children; they didn't know what marriage was. When they grew up, they could not say no to their marriage, so they got married."

"So why did you give my mother to my father when she was eight years old," Murad asked innocently.

"I told you, I am a woman, I have no control over giving a daughter to a husband. No woman has such control, only men, the fathers have the power to get their children married to anyone they wish."

Murad was quiet for a long while.

"Your mother was the subject of a bet of the wishbone game."

"What?"

"Yes, the bet of a wishbone game. Do you know the wishbone game?"

"Yes. But how my mother was the bet of this game?

"I don't know grandma, what the wishbone game is, tell me what is it?" inquired Zarin, who was also listening to the conversation.

"The wishbone game is like this." Grandmother put her hands over the heads of her grandchildren one by one. "Every chicken has a bone called the wishbone, which looks like this," the grandmother raised her right hand with index and middle fingers opened in a V shape. "The two people, who want to play this game, should determine the subject or bet of the game first like money or clothing or something else. Then each person holds one leg of the wishbone, pull them apart until it breaks into two pieces, then the game begins. If one of the two persons hands over a thing to the other person and the other person fails to say "I remember" and also the first person says "I remembered, you forgot" in this case the second person is the loser and should give the bet of the game to the first person."

The old lady hesitated, then continued. "It was your grandfather– my husband– may God bless him and grant him a stay in Heaven– who was playing the wishbone game with your father's father, may God bless him. They were neighbors in Maimana. One time they had a dispute over a piece of land located between their houses. They fought and became enemies over that piece of land. One day, the leaders of the Uzbek tribe and the *Augho* or Pashtun tribe decided to reconcile your grandfathers with each other. They invited them to a dinner party in the house of Baqir Bi, who was a good and rich man from my Uzbek tribe. He invited all the government people such as the governor of Faryab, the police commander, the mayor of Maimana and so many other big government officials and other important people to the party. Your father's father," the grandmother pointed to Murad, "got the wishbone in his part of the chicken meat at dinner, and said to my husband: "Let's break the wishbone," Your other grandfather agreed but asked: "What is the bet of the game?" Your father's father said: "You see, my friend, I have sons and daughters and you have sons and daughters too. If I win, you give your older daughter to my son, if you win; I give my older daughter to your older son. The whole party liked the idea, saying this way the two families will become relatives, and there will be no more disputes and fighting between them."

Both children were staring at their grandma with their mouths open.

"It was one week later," continued Grandmother, "that both of your grandfathers were together in the mosque for prayer. After the prayer, they were discussing something when your mother's father, my husband, liked the *tasbeh* that your other grandfather had in his hand, and said, 'Oh brother, you got such a beautiful *Tasbeh,* where did you get them from?' And your father's father replied while handing over the t*asbeh* to him: 'A friend of mine brought me this *Tasbeh* from Mecca.' And then he quickly said: 'I remembered, you forgot!' And everyone around there saw it, so that was it. And my husband said, 'Okay, you won. My daughter Madina can be married to your son.' Soon after that, there waw a ceremony with the participation of many people and the mullah, where Sakhidad's father granted the Sweets to your father's father."

Grandmother took a deep breath of relief, hoping Murad was satisfied with her answer and would stop asking her more questions.

But Murad was far from satisfied. Grandma's answer created more questions to him. He and Zarin looked at each other with great curiosity.

"What is Sweets grandma?" Asked both children simultaneously.

"Sweets is like a platter full of candies that the father of the girl gives to the father of the boy in the meaning that the deal was done and could not be reversed."

"How old was my mother at that time?" asked Murad.

"She was only eight years old, and your father was eleven. But your mother went to your father's house when she was 14 years old."

"How much money did his grandfather give to you for your daughter?" Zarin asked innocently.

"You mean dowry? No, there was no dowry. We had no money because Sakhidad's father lost the wishbone game, so there was no money given to us. We gave his mother to his father for free. Maybe that's why she was ill-fated, and Murad's father didn't like her because he did not spend money for bringing her to his home. Now, you kids go do your prayer and then go to your beds, it's late in the night," Grandmother announced with a sense of relief. She got up to perform the nightly prayer and then went to bed.

During his long work days, Murad was mostly quiet, trying to avoid having discussions with Ghulam for the fear that he might again bring up the issue of parents and their tribal affiliations. He tried to make himself busy with his work and even do things that were not his responsibility, such as washing dishes, refilling the water in the *Samawat* early in the morning, and taking the ashes of the charcoal out. The factor that was adding up to his loneliness was that he was not allowed by his uncle to have simple chats with the customers, not to pair up with boys next door in the bazaar. He was repeatedly cautioned about the danger of *Bachabazi*, and forbidden to get friendly with any man older than him.

In the midst of all his disappointments, loneliness and lack of self-esteem, the only place and time where Murad could feel a bit comfortable, was his uncle's house at night. His grandmother was a kind lady; she loved both him and Zarin. She was particularly kind to Murad as the orphan child of her ill-fated deceased daughter.

The other person with whom he felt comfortable was his cousin-Zarin. Zarin did not care about Murad's humiliating parental heritage. The 13-year-old girl was pretty, kind, funny and open-minded. Usually at night, when Sakhidad was gone to his bedroom, the two children would listen to their grandmother, who would tell them interesting folk stories. But after the old lady had been gone to her bed too, Murad and Zarin would stay awake and play the *hiding fist* games, and tell riddles and enigmas. Zarin would sometimes make fun of her cousin. After a while, the two youngsters started wrestling with each other. Murad was careful and would try to keep the noise down, so his uncle and grandmother didn't hear. One night Zarin tried to twist Murad's arm, he resisted, and when trying to twist her arm, he touched one of Zarin's nipples by accident. Murad apologized, but Zarin ignored it as if nothing had happened.

Playing with pretty Zarin gradually injected some ideas and wishes into Murad's mind. He could not sleep for hours even though he and Zarin were chatting and playing until midnight. Zarin slept with her grandmother, and Murad slept in a separate room, close to the gate of the mud house, that was normally used as a guest room.

Playing every night with Zarin, made him think that she was also interested in him, or at least she would not complain to her father or grandmother if he gets a bit intimate, Murad suggested to Zarin the idea of playing the wishbone game with each other.

Zarin agreed but asked what would be the bet of the game.

"If I lose, I will give you five Afghanis. Now you tell me what you would give me if you lose?" asked Murad.

"I don't know; you tell me what you want from me if I lose? Oh yes" exclaimed Zarin. "I too can give you five Afghanis, if I lose."

"You don't have money,"

"I do. My dad gives me two Afghanis every week; now I have ten Afghanis savings."

"No. I don't want money; you give me something deferent."

"Ummm, I can weave you a threaded hat. Grandma just showed me how to weave the hat."

"I have two hats, don't need another one."

"So what do you want? You don't want money or a hat, then what do you want from me, if I lose?" exclaimed Zarin.

Murad turned away from her, covered his face with both of his hands.

"A kiss," he whispered and ran to his bedroom to sleep.

Zarin frowned, followed by a sweet smile.

Once in his bed, Murad was feeling the warmth of Zarin's nipple, feeling the same as hard and as warm as the knob at the top of the teapot that they were using for cooking *Chainaki* in it in the teahouse. From now on, his life found a new meaning; his imagination would run wilder and wilder every night. He was encouraged even to think of ways to make Zarin his life mate.

He wished he could play the wishbone game with his uncle as he knew he would never be able to afford to pay 20,000 to 50,000 Afghanis as dowry if he was to get married, let alone to afford the expenses of the wedding. So he was dreaming of winning the wishbone game from his uncle and get his hand on his daughter. He was willing to work for his uncle for the rest of his life in the event he lost the game.

"Murad looks happier these days." Ghulam shared the fact with his boss.

"Yes," Sakhidad agreed. "I promised him to buy him a new coat for the upcoming winter. I will buy you one too."

"Thank you," said Ghulam in a low voice. He was not sure, however, if that was the true reason for Murad's happiness. Ghulam had been, from the very beginning, concealing his concern over Murad's arrival to Andkhoy and his living in Sakhidad's house. Besides being worried about Zarin, he didn't like Murad because he was seeing him as a potential rival for his lead position in the busyness. But he was cautious in the meantime not to create a situation for his boss. He remembered Sakhidad mentioned to him time and again that Murad was a good kid, that his mother had been his good sister and that he felt for Murad as her sister's orphan child who was not treated well by his father either.

Murad, on the other hand, was feeling friendly toward Ghulam at the beginning but gradually looked at him as a rival. He did developed, however, jealousy toward him as after working hard for over a year and a half, he still wasn't trusted by his uncle to do the money part of the busyness or even touch the register. He once heard from Ghulam that he was getting paid 50 Afghanis a week, five times as much as he was. Likewise, unlike Ghulam, he was never trusted with shopping for things for the teahouse such as sugar, candy, tea, bread and so on. Even though he was a couple of years younger than Ghulam, he was doing harder jobs and doing more things in the teahouse than him.

"Why that motorcycle guy eats two *chainakies* each time he comes in?" Murad asked Ghulam in a friendly tone, referring to one of the customers, who rode a motorcycle and would usually show up for lunch or sometimes for dinner once or twice a month.

"Because he is smoking hashish, hashish makes one hungry," answered Ghulam also in a friendly tone.

Murad was quiet for a moment.

"How come the three of us eat only one *chainaki* at lunch time?" asked Murad hesitantly, meaning his uncle, Ghulam and himself.

"Because your uncle wants to save money,"

"But you said hashish makes everyone hungry, he smokes hashish too, right?"

"Yes. But I told you your uncle wants to save money; he adds up more water and bread to the meal. Ghulam looked out through the exit door of the teahouse making sure Sakhidad was not around and added: "He wants to save money for his wedding."

"Who's wedding?" asked Murad, hoping Ghulam's answer would be: "Yours. Your and Zarin's wedding."

"His own wedding," replied Ghulam with a smile. "With my sister," he added quickly and cheerfully.

Murad was surprised. His mouth stayed open for a second. Sakhidad came in, and the two boys went after their daily duties.

Murad now realized that why Ghulam was so trusted in the business and why he was so close to his uncle. He remembered his uncle saying to him that Ghulam was a good boy, and required that they should get along well with each other. Therefore, from now on, Murad was cautious in dealing with him and tried not to show his feelings of rivalry towards him. Actually, he was somehow happy for knowing this because he thought besides being coworkers, Ghulam was going to be his relative as well.

Murad continued to work hard and perform duties that were not even his responsibilities to please Ghulam because from now on, he was seeing him as a friend and a future relative. He even one time contemplated sharing with him his secret that he was in love with his cousin Zarin. But the fear that he might tell his uncle about it, kept him from so doing.

The issue of his uncle's marriage with Ghulam's sister occupied his mind and had many questions about Ghulam's sister's age, the amount of dowry his uncle paid or would have to pay to Ghulam's stepfather, about the timing of the wedding and so on.

Two weeks later, when Sakhidad went out of the teahouse for personal business, Ghulam initiated a conversation with Murad.

"Didn't your uncle tell you about his wedding?"

"No. He never talked to me about it."

"What does he talk to you about at home or when you walk home?"

"Nothing, he just talks about work," answered Murad. "You can see, in the night before we go home, he smokes hashish, he is silent all the way to home. At home, we, grandma and his daughter eat dinner together soon after we get there. He doesn't talk much with them either. After the dinner, he does his ablution and prayer and then goes to his room and sleeps. How old is your sister?" Murad asked, using this opportunity to have Ghulam talk about his sister.

"She will be fourteen in four months."

Murad went to a longer silence.

"Do you know how old your uncle is?" asked Ghulam.

"I was thinking about the same thing," replied Murad. "My mother had said he was two years older than she was."

"How old was your mother when she died?"

"Forty-one."

Both boys did the calculation. Sakhidad was forty-five.

"When is the wedding?" asked Murad.

"Maybe soon, after my sister turns fourteen, and your uncle has enough money for the wedding."

"How much was the dowry?"

"Very much."

"How much?"

"I can't tell you now."

Murad paused again for a while.

"Why fourteen? Why isn't he marrying now?" Murad asked.

"My stepfather and your uncle said that both girls should be wedded after they turned fourteen?"

"Both girls? Who is the other girl?" Murad asked himself, but before he could ask Ghulam, Sakhidad entered the teahouse and Ghulam put his index finger on his lips."Cheshsh,"

Murad was puzzled by what he heard. "Who was the other girl who was going to be wedded when turns fourteen? How old is Zarin? Is Zarin already engaged with someone?"

That night at home, Murad decided to ask grandmother. She knew everything. His uncle went to his bedroom, but Zarin was still there. He was hesitant to share his concerns with Zarin, so he waited until she stepped out for something, then he hurriedly asked his grandmother.

"Grandma, how old is Zarin?"

"Thirteen," Grandmother answered without thinking for a second.

"Are you and uncle giving her to a husband?" Murad felt bashful asking the question.

"You know son; she is in the name of Ghulam, the boy who works with you."

Murad's eyes flickered with surprise and felt a sharp pain in his skull.

"Ghulam has so much money for the dowry?" Panic stormed in Murad's mind.

"There is no dowry, son. Zarin and Ghulam's sister are an exchange deal."

"What, what is exchange deal?"

"Ghulam's sister will be your uncle's wife, and Zarin will be Ghulam's wife with no money or dowry, understand now?"

Murad was faint, his mouth went open and stayed like that for a while. For him, the puzzle was solved, and he was identified to be the loser. When Zarin returned to the room, he announced that he had a headache, and left the room.

The grandma felt for Murad. She had realized lately that Murad liked Zarin; she would be happy actually to see her two orphan grandchildren married to each other and staying with her in the house. But it was too late.

The next night, the old lady noticed that Murad was pale, his lips were dry, and his face was furrowed. She tried to talk to him about his day at work, and keep him in the room while looking for an opportunity to get alone with him.

"You know son," she said when they were by themselves in the room, "this happened before you came to Andkhoy. Had you been here before that, I would have talked to Sakhidad to give Zarin to you, so you both could live with me here. But you don't be sad, God is great, I will find you another girl here."

Murad was now sadder than before as he realized that there was no way to reverse this deal, but still, could not help to demonstrate his wishes to his grandmother further.

"Zarin likes me too," he said.

"No, don't say that son, your uncle will be very mad, he will kick you out of this house. I know he will do that. I know you have nowhere to go. For God sake, don't say that to anyone, okay?" The grandmother said with a deep anxiousness. "If he realizes that Zarin likes you, I am afraid he is going even to kill her."

When Zarin returned to the room, she had no idea what was being said about her. She invited Murad to tell riddles as usual. But the grandmother came to his rescue. "Murad has a little headache," she said. "I will give him some aspirin and send him to bed. You two can play tomorrow night."

Murad's old feeling of jealousy and revelry towards Ghulam resurfaced all at once, and gradually turned into hate. He could no longer entertain himself with sweet fantasies, and with dreaming of having a future with Zarin. But instead, he was daydreaming and constantly making his mind occupied with the plans for beating Ghulam, removing him from the job and even killing him.

"Tell your father that you want to marry me, not Ghulam." Murad imagined telling Zarin and having her to announce to her father. But he recalled his grandmother saying that "Sakhidad would kill the girl". He would then feel dizzy.

It did not take longer for Ghulam to realize that Murad hated him. It was mutual. He was certain that Murad has eyes on Zarin. Ghulam also thought that Murad finally found out, either from his grandmother or Zarin herself that Zarin was going to be his wife.

There was a fierce silent antagonism going on between the two young men. Murad was still desperately hoping for something drastic to happen. Or someone coming forward telling him that there was still a way that he could be Zarin's husband.

By the passing of every day, Murad felt lonely and lost hope for his uncle's help. Even though he became certain that his grandmother couldn't do anything for him, he still was thinking of her as his best confident and wished to get a good advice from her.

"Did Zarin ever met Ghulam?" Murad asked one night when alone with Grandmother.

"No son. No," said grandmother with emphasis. "You know, in our religion, they are not husband and wife until a mullah performs the *Nikah* in the presence of two witnesses, and according to our traditions and customs, they cannot meet and talk to each other before that."

"If Zarin says she doesn't want to marry Ghulam, what will happen?" Murad could not help to show his extreme eagerness toward Zarin.

"She can't say that. I told you her father will kill her!" The voice of the old lady cracked as she tried to emphasize her point.

"Why?"

"Because if she doesn't want to marry Ghulam, your uncle is going to lose his future wife, Ghulam's sister. He cannot afford to pay a dowry for a wife and find such a young girl again in his whole life. Be very careful, son. If he finds out that you like her, he might kill you too."

That night, Murad went to bed with maddening feelings of disappointment. "It looks like everyone is now my enemy," thought

Murad. Lately, both his uncle and Ghulam appeared to be frowning at him all day, even though he was doing his job right. Ghulam tried not to talk to him except when giving him orders for doing things. He would sometimes even criticized him for little tiny issues. Unlike before, Sakhisdad would call him Murad or *boy*, instead of calling him son.

"Haven't you heard from your little brothers and sister, how are they doing?" Sakhidad asked Murad one night when they were walking home from work.

"No, uncle."

"You should go to visit them. It has been a long time since you have been here. I heard your father is very sick."

Murad became certain that he could no longer stay and work with his uncle. "Where could he go?" He would repeatedly ask himself. At home, Zarin's attitude toward him changed. She stopped playing with him. After eating dinner, she would get up to do abolition, perform the nightly prayer and go to her bed. During the short while before going to bed, she would try to avoid looking at him and sit away from him. The grandmother was anxious too, she would announce the sleeping time to him and Zarin just a few minutes after they ate dinner, so there will be no time for them to talk or play with each other.

"What happened, grandma, no one is talking to me anymore?" Murad said humbly one night as Zarin was still in the room.

"Your uncle doesn't like you and Zarin playing and talking to each other."

"He told you?"

"Yes, he overheard you two whispering to each other. He doesn't like it." *Ana* looked at him with sympathy. "I am very much concerned about you. You know, your uncle is going to be very bad to you someday if you are still here."

"What can I do? Where can I go, Grandma?" asked Murad with desperation, looking at Zarin for empathy. *Ana* pointed to Zarin to go to her bed and then replied:

"Go to your home, to your father."

"I cannot live with my stepmother; she is a very bad woman. Had I had the money or a good job, I would have taken my brothers and sister out of that house too."

"Yes, go find another job." Grandmother suddenly paused, as if she had just remembered something. "Aha, you know son, you can work in a smithy shop. You have experience in the job, right?"

"Yes, but work where?"

"The neighbor at the beginning of two streets from ours is a blacksmith, he has a smithy shop in the town, and your uncle knows him. I will tell him to talk to the guy; maybe he will give you a job."

"Where can I live?"

"Maybe you can stay with the blacksmith for a while and later on you can rent a room for yourself in the *caravansary*– the travelers' lodging. It's cheap. Oh, you know? I remember that the blacksmith has no children; he has one daughter who is married. Maybe he will let you stay in his house forever."

Murad was silent for a while. "Can you talk to uncle tonight to talk to the smith?"

"I will talk to him tomorrow night before he goes to his bedroom."

Murad liked that idea. He would be living in the same town where Zarin was and could see her whenever he will be paying visits to the grandmother.

"Why don't you go back to your father?" Ghulam asked Murad in an antagonistic tone the next day when Sakhidad was out, and there were no customers in the teahouse.

"This is none of your business, you jerk," Murad didn't bother hiding his anger.

"If I am a jerk, you are a donkey," said Ghulam.

Murad gazed at Ghulam, squeezing his lips and right fist as if ready to punch him in the face. "You call me a donkey?"

"Yes, you are a donkey."

Murad punched Ghulam in the face.

"If it were not for my father-in-law, I would have smashed your teeth, you dog," Ghulam shouted.

"Your father-in-law?" asked Murad angrily.

"Yes, my father in- law! I am his son-in-law, and will be living with him after the wedding," cried Ghulam victoriously, "I don't want to see you around the!"

Murad was about to hit Ghulam again when the motorcyclist customer, the hash smoker who ate two *Chainakies* by himself, came into the teahouse for early lunch. He sensed that the two boys were having a fight, said hi to both and asked for a fresh hookah with two *chainakies* to follow.

Before going out to the patio for a smoke, the man sat down on the mattress, called Murad and pointed to his hands. Murad brought a *gadwa* and *dastshoy* in a hurry to wash the customer's hands.

"Hello Murad, my name is Rustam Khan, why were you two fighting?" Whispered the customer as Murad started pouring water over his hands.

"He doesn't want me to work anymore with my uncle,"

"Why?"

"He is my enemy, I cannot work here anymore," Murad said in a low voice.

"So what would you be doing if you leave here, and how old are you?"

"Sixteen," said Murad.

"You are too young for my work. A little bit more time, I will have a good job for you, God willing," said Rustam in a low voice so that Ghulam, who was busy with fanning the charcoal fire, wouldn't hear.

"What Job?"

"It's a hard job for you now. I will tell you some other time, God willing. But what are you going to do now?"

"I don't know. My grandmother said there is a smithy shop in the bazaar here; I can work there if the guy hires me."

"Do you know the job?"

"Yes, my father is a blacksmith; I worked with him in the past."

"Good, I know that blacksmith, his name is Mansur. I will talk to him about you this afternoon, God willing."

Murad thanked Rustam Khan.

The next morning, he went to *Hamam*– a local public bath, as he would usually do every two weeks. *Hamam* was the only place where he could wash his whole body, and have a larger mirror on the wall in the lobby to freely look at himself. For the first time in his life, Murad felt proud of himself as a man, mature enough to mingle with other men as he examined his newly grown beard and mustache. He looked at his beard and mustache from different angles in the mirror and combed them with his fingers several times. Then he shaved the hair on the fronts of his cheeks from temple to temple as to make his beard appear more vivid.

"Nobody can now think of me as a *bacha berish*– a boy subject to sexual favor. "I can now mingle with other men, I am a man myself!" he announced to himself.

After returning to the teahouse, Murad attracted the attention of his uncle and Ghulam as he looked clean, well groomed, but more importantly, mannish. The two blinked at each other with smiles but said nothing. Murad noticed, said nothing and went to his daily routine.

"Are you getting married or what? You are so well groomed!" Asked Rustam Khan jokingly, who come for lunch again and asked Murad to wash his hands?

"No sir, nobody gives me their daughter."

"Why not, I can find you a good girl, after you start working with me, God willing."

Two days later in the morning, Sakhidad left for the teahouse by himself without saying goodbye to Murad. Murad then said goodbye to Zarin, and his grandmother left their home and waited in front of the house for Rustam Khan to arrive and take him to Mansur's shop.

"Mansur is my friend, he is a good man and will take care of you, God willing" Rustam Khan told Murad while giving him a ride to Mansur's shop on the back seat of his motorcycle.

"I will work hard for him," Murad assured Rustam Khan.

"Ok, I will be checking on you time to time to see how you are doing."

"Thank you, Khan Sahib."

The shop was located only twenty minutes' walk from his uncle's teahouse and only 30 minutes' walk to Mansur's home. His deal with Mansur was that he would be working from sunrise to sunset, Saturday through Thursday, as the shop was closed on Friday. For the first two months, he would be getting paid 30 Afghanis per week, because the business was slow at the time. The pay might increase afterward if the business picked up. Murad would be paying 50 Afghanis a month for his room in Mansur's mud house. He was eating with Mansur and his wife for free.

Mansur liked Murad. Here again, he proved to be a hard and dedicated worker. In the morning, he was always ready to go to work as soon as Mansur was. They would walk together between work and home. He was happy with the job, but the only thing that was bothering him was that Mansur's wife was asking him too many questions about his family. Every night after eating dinner, she would question him that why he wasn't living with his father and that why he stopped working with his uncle. His answers were brief and tried to keep silent so that she would leave him alone.

Customers were happy with the job Murad was doing at the smithy shop; in four or five months there was an increase in the number of customers. On Fridays, he would usually pay a visit to his uncle's teahouse and then to his grandmother and Zarin. But it changed after Zarin and Ghulam got married, he was not invited the wedding and did not even know when the wedding occurred until one Friday that he knocked on his uncle's house and was met by his grandmother at the door.

"Ghulam is home son, he is now living with us, and maybe he doesn't want you to come in. Your uncle also said one day that Zarin was not allowed to reveal her face to you as she is now a married woman."

His grandmother did not even invite him to the guestroom for a cup of tea, but briefly said goodbye to him at the front door. Murad remembered at the same time that Ghulam had already prohibited him from going into Sakhidad's house after his and Zarin's wedding.

Murad had lost his first love with no hope for another one. He lost the family connection with his grandmother, his uncle and his cousin.

In the meantime, he was concerned about his young brothers and sister who were subject to the cruel treatment by their stepmother and heartless father. Dangerous thoughts, even the idea of suicide, were invading his mind time to time. By the passage of time, the agony of destitution caused by losing his love and family connection had deteriorated as Mansur fell sick and died after three months of illness.

Mansur's wife of 62, one year younger than her husband, decided to move in with her daughter who was living in the Shagley village over 50 kilometers away. Mansur's wife struck a deal with Murad and leased the shop to him for 300 Afghanis net payment per month. Murad was also responsible for the house rent- 200 Afghanis per month.

Murad agreed and would pay a total of 500 Afghanis to Mansur's wife. She would travel from Shagley to downtown Andkhoy every month only to collect the money from Murad.

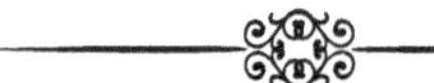

Murad pinned his hopes on his business. He hired another person from the neighborhood as a helper. He was, in the meantime, dreaming about bringing his brothers and sister to work and live with him. But by the end of the first year of his ownership, he was not able to make payments to Mansur's wife. Two months after stopping the payment, Mansur's wife was very angry at him.

"If you don't pay me the money in one week, I am going to take you to the police station," she shouted at him.

Murad was terrified by the threat of being taken to the police station. He still had the memory of the police station in Maimana, where he was detained for stealing a live chicken. He remembered the way the police there treated him and the other detainee. But he had no way of making money and paying his dues. One time he thought of asking his uncle for help but could not afford the disgrace of Ghulam and Zarin knowing his situation.

One of the neighbors on the street owned a motorcycle, which he thought of stealing it. On the back of the motorcycle, he could escape Andkhoy, and sell the motorcycle somewhere else, come back to

Andkhoy, hire someone to kill Ghulam so that he could start working with his uncle again and get married to Zarin.

Mansur's wife ran out of patience and gave Murad two days to pay, or she would complain to the police. He was hoping that Rustam Khan comes by and ask him for help, but Rustam Khan had not paid a visit to Murad's shop for two or three weeks, which was unusual for him. He did not know how and where to contact Rustam Khan.

Mansur's wife did what she had promised she would- taking Murad to the police station over the money he owed her. Murad was humiliated and beaten in the police station. He was jailed again in a room much like the one in Maimana almost five years ago.

As desperate he was, toward the middle of the night, Murad initiated a conversation with his guarding policeman begging him to release him, he would leave Andkhoy forever, and pay him the 200 Afghanis, that he had spared for himself, in return.

"Do you swear you will disappear forever?" The policeman asked.

"I swear to God I will leave Andkhoy tonight and never come back."

"If you were seen in Andkhoy, I would be in trouble, and I swear to God I will kill you."

"Yes I swear, you will never see me again in Andkhoy," promised Murad.

"You know, I have only one month left for my service as a policeman here, but I am sure *Sarmamoor* Sahib will not believe me that you gave me only 200 Afghanis, so go ahead, search all your pockets, because this is nothing."

"I swear to God I have only 50 Afghanis more, with which money I have to get myself to Maimana."

The policeman decided not to let Murad go because the 200 Afghanis he offered was nothing for taking the risk of releasing him. Murad nearly cried out of desperation.

"I swear to God if I had a thousand Afghanis, I would have given it to you," Murad groaned.

"Your 200 is nothing," said the policeman, but before leaving the room, he paused and listened to the sound of a motorcycle engine that came closer and closer to the police station and then stopped. The policeman sneaked out of the room and saw a shadow.

"Who is this?" called the policeman to the person on the back of his motorcycle.

"Barath, is that you? I am Rustam Kha!"

"Oh, Salaam, Rustam Khan. What are you doing here?"

"They told me that you brought Murad here, right?"

"Yes, he owes money to a woman, and *Sarmamoor* Sahib ordered me to keep him here a few days."

"I want to see him."

"Okay," said the policeman, running to the room. He returned with Murad, his hands cuffed in the back.

"Salaam, Kahn sahib," said Murad to Rustam Khan loudly but trying to sound as sad as possible.

"Salaam Murad, stay here tonight. I will talk to *Sarmamoor* sahib tomorrow and ask him to release you by my guarantee, God willing."

"God bless you Khan Sahib," Murad replied, disappointed by the fact that his hands were tied and was not able to kiss Khan's hand.

"Don't bother him, let him sleep tonight, I will talk to *Sarmamoor* sahib tomorrow morning, God Willing," said Rustam Khan to the policeman, starting his motorcycle's ignition.

"Will do Khan Sahib," said the policeman.

Rustam Khan left. And the policeman said to Murad with extreme astonishment: "Oh man, I had no idea that you were such an important guy that you know Rustam Khan, and you are close to him so much that he wants to release you from jail!"

"Yes, I have known him for a long time," Murad said, feeling greatly triumphant. "How do you know him?"

"Well, he is a friend of the *sarmamoor* sahib. He comes here a lot to meet with him. He is a rich man, and has a lot of people behind him," The policeman said, nodding approvingly several times.

Murad realized that Rustam Khan was the only person who could help him, so he tried not to ask the policeman more questions who was already convinced that he was a close fellow of Khan.

The next morning, Rustam showed up on his motorcycle as soon as the chief of police came into his office. He said Salaam to and shook hands with Rustam Khan who was waiting in front of his office.

"Salaam, Khan Sahib, how come I see you here in the early morning?" The police chief asked while still holding Rustam Khan's hand in his.

"Yes, *Sarmamoor* sahib, I am here for my boy, Murad. He is going to be someone useful to us, to you and me in the future," Rustam answered with a little wink. Then a whisper got exchanged between the two, and then the police chief ordered his soldier to let Murad go with Rustam Khan.

Murad rode with Rustam Khan on the back seat of his motorcycle, leaving the police station in a hurry.

"Khan Sahib, do you live out of town?" Asked Murad wondering why he was driving so far out of the town.

"I have a *Qala*-in the village, with a house and a factory in it," Answered Rustam Khan.

"A factory?" Murad wondered.

"Yes, a factory of making home-made cloth washing soap. You will be working there."

"Why do you have a factory out of town?"

"Because I have a big house there with no neighbors to complain about the odor of the soap."

Murad believed him.

"You don't like to go out of town?" Rustam asked Murad.

"I want to see my grandmother sometimes here in town," Murad said in a low voice.

"No. I know you want to see Zarin sometimes, right? I know that. But you know you cannot see her anymore as she is now married to Ghulam, and you are not allowed to their house anymore. But still, don't worry we will be coming to the town, God Willing, I have a house here in the town too."

"Is your family living here in the town?" asked Murad enthusiastically.

"Yes."

At the arrival to the gate of *Qala*-castle– a huge structure with tall mud walls, Rustam blew his motorcycle's horn three times, and the heavy wooden gate with metal straps at the length and the width opened. The two doormen, with colorful caps, quilted robes, and belts around their waists, said Salaam-peace be upon you, to them, raising their hands in a soldierly gesture and let them in.

"They don't look *augho*," said Murad to himself looking at their outfits. "Their faces and noses and foreheads all look like my uncle's." He was a little concerned about their as well as Rustam's tribal identity.

Rustam, around his early 40s, was a strong figure with heavy shoulders, well dressed in local Uzbek *chapan*-quilted robe, a colorful cap, cotton trousers, narrowed at the ankles, and high boots. He also looked like a mixture of *augho* and Uzbek, which was a cause of comfort to Murad.

"Let's go see my castle," Rustam said.

He first took Murad to a small living room, furnished with Afghan hand-made rugs, and mattresses and pillows stuffed with cotton, covered with burgundy velvet fabric.

"This is where we all sometimes sleep that we have to be here in the night," explained Rustam.

"This is the storage for the soap- making materials, and this is the soap- making machine." Rustam showed Murad two other rooms one after another.

"What is in there?" asked Murad, pointing to another structure behind the soap making room. It looked abandoned.

"I will show you that place later, let's drink some tea, we are tired."

Murad followed Rustam to the furnished room. Rustam took his cap off his head and placed it next to him on the mattress.

"He is working here too." Rustam pointed to an older man in his early 50s, who just entered the room with a tray containing a teapot, teacups, saucers, and a crystal bowl full of sugar cubes. "His name is Mahmood, he and the other man you saw at the gate- Qurban Ali are good men, they work for me," Rustam added.

Mahmood poured the tea and placed the cup in front of Murad.

"Thank you," Murad said while still looking around the nicely furnished room.

"Do you know how to cook?" Mahmood asked Murad jokingly.

"He can cook *chainaki*," answered Rustam for him.

"Oh good, now we can eat delicious *chainaki*," said Mahmood. Everyone smiled.

"You and I will be traveling to Almar district sometime soon, God willing, and also maybe every two or three months we will be traveling to the south of the country," said Rustam, laying his right elbow over the pillow next to him.

Murad gazed at him, wondering what he meant by the south of the country.

"We will go to Farah, and also to Helmand province if needed, to obtain material for our factory, God willing."

"Have you gone there before?" Murad wondered why they would have to go that far to buy materials for soap.

"Yes, I go there once every two–three months," answered Rustam, nodding, "Nowadays our business is getting larger, we get new customers even from outside of our country, like Iran and Turkmenistan. We might need to buy a Russian jeep, God willing. I want you to learn driving."

Despite a bit of uncertainty, Murad was seeing an opportunity for himself in working with Rustam. But he wanted to know why he was going to be chosen for the trips, not those old employees who might have been more reliable and trustworthy to Rustam.

"Have they been to Farah and Helmand?" asked Murad, pointing toward the exit door, referring to the two men.

Rustam paused a second. "They are old," he said. "You know Murad, first of all, I have watched you for the past almost four years when you were working for your uncle and then working with Mansur. I got a lot of information about you from your uncle. He told me about how your father was treating you, he told me about your small brothers and sister. I found you to be a good hardworking person. You are one I can trust. Also, your face looks like the people in the South. They might be good to you when doing business with them."

"But my grandmother said they are *augho*; they speak another language."

"You are *augho* too. Don't worry; you will learn their language soon, God willing. They understand this Farsi language too that you and I are speaking."

"What about the money I owe to Mansur's wife?" Murad asked worriedly.

"I will take care of that soon."

But Murad had another, bigger worry:

"Maybe in a year or so I will be asked for my military service," said Murad anxiously.

"I know, Murad. I thought about that. We will do something about it when the time comes, God willing."

"Like what?"

"As I said, when the time comes, I will tell you how I will take care of this issue God willing," Rustam repeated.

"If nothing else, I can bring you here to Andkhoy to do your service period as a policeman, God willing."

"Can you do that Khan Sahib?" Murad asked with extreme enthusiasm.

"Yes, Murad. You don't know me; with the help of God, I can do anything I want." Rustam sipped his tea, emptying the cup. "Let's go out to the field; I will show you how to drive the motorcycle, God willing."

Murad tried learning how to drive Rustam's 175 CC Honda Motorcycle for an hour, Rustam Khan praised him for being a quick learner.

"That's enough for today; you are going to become a good driver soon, God willing. Let's eat; I am hungry.

So far, Murad liked the idea of working with Rustam, hoping he will save money for his future and to help his brothers and sister. He was especially delighted because his debt to Mansur's wife would be taken care of. But still, one very important question remained unanswered. He was shy to ask Rustam that question, thinking it might bother him and make him change his mind.

"We may be going to Almar District in a few days, God willing," Rustam announced.

"What will be my job here?" Murad was willing to start working right away.

"I will tell you about that when we return from Almar, God willing. I want you mostly to be traveling with me as my driver. That's why I want you to learn how to drive the motorcycle. You will be driving a Russian jeep when I buy one maybe in a few months, God willing." Rustam talked in an authoritative tone. "One thing I want to tell you which is very important is that you never miss your five-time daily prayer. In the prayer, there is a blessing of God, both in this world and in the world after the resurrection. If you do your prayer all the times, God will put His blessing into all your life, and your business will thrive. You will be successful in every endeavor, and you will be secure from all disasters, God willing."

Murad listened to his new boss attentively, nodding affirmatively.

Rustam called on his two servants who were busy doing their routine, that it was time for the afternoon prayer. All four of them did their ablution and then performed the afternoon prayer in assembly, with Rustam acting as Imam.

"You and they will be sleeping in this room, so you guys will not get bored. Sometimes I sleep here too. It's not cold yet, next month we will buy wood chips for the stove. But today you are going with me to see my house, and tomorrow we go to find Mansur's wife to take care of your debts."

Rustam and Murad left the castle for the town in the evening.

That night, Rustam directed Murad to a guest room in his big house. It was a well-furnished room. For the first time in his life, Murad was staying in a two-story house with brick and stone walls. The room was clean; the whole house was nicely painted. There was running water from a tank over a well in the house. He could listen to a battery-operated radio in his room. And there was a lady servant working in the house, doing all the cleaning and cooking. Rustam's parents also had a room on the first floor, but Rustam himself lived on the second floor along with his wife and two children, both girls under 10.

In the next two days, Murad practiced more driving the motorcycle.

"You are a good driver now," Rustam said. "Let's go to Shagley village to give the money to Mansur's wife. You drive." Rustam commanded Murad in the morning and handed over to him his motorcycle's key.

Murad drove to the Shagley village without making any mistakes; Rustam praised him for that. They found Mansur's wife and gave her whatever money Murad owed her.

"Tomorrow morning we leave for Almar early in the dark right after the Morning Prayer, God willing. Be ready," Rustam instructed Murad, after dinner. "We are going to my castle now, and leave for Almar from there God willing."

In the castle, Rustam, Murad, and the two servants performed the nightly prayer; then the servers prepared four beds; throwing four mattresses side by side in the room and putting pillows at the edge of the mattresses one for each person.

"Get up everyone, perform your prayer," Rustam called on everyone in the room, drying his arms with his *dopata* at 4 AM.

Murad was the first to get up. He went out to do his ablution. In a little while, all got together for Morning Prayer in assembly with Rustam acting as Imam.

Their breakfast was brief; black tea with home cooked bread and two boiled eggs each person. Soon after sipping his last drop of black tea, Rustam loaded a middle size shabby leather luggage at the track of his motorcycle, and by 5 AM he and Murad were on the motorcycle, roaring toward their destination. In less than an hour, they were out of the Andkhoy District and halfway the Qaramqul district. When they arrived at the desert, Rustam stopped the motorcycle.

"How are you doing young man?" Rustam asked Murad.

"I am good Khan Sahib."

"Get the key, now you drive. Be careful, if you see a Russian jeep anywhere along the way, stop." Rustam took a pair of binoculars out from under his robe and got on the back seat. "You know, police sometimes stop everyone driving on the way, they are wasting our time if you see them I want you to stop then I will drive to avoid them."

After driving for an hour, and after they passed the district of Dawlatabad, Rustam praised Murad for driving fast and driving ably. "*Mashallah*, you drive well."

While enjoying the compliments he received from his boss and trying his utmost to drive the motorcycle as careful as he could, Murad was in the meantime watchful of the surrounding of the road as farther as possible because he was scared of the police. Therefore, he was able to spot a police jeep following them from a distance of about a couple of kilometers. He quickly alerted Rustam Khan and carefully pulled over to the side of the road.

"Khan Sahib, I think that is a police jeep running after us!" he said pointing to a cyclone behind them.

Rustam saw the Russian jeep through his binoculars and quickly took the over the driving. He was driving as fast as possible along the rugged terrain for almost two hours. It was daylight now, and before arriving in the district of Almar, they could see a dark dust following them from the right side of the desert like a crazy horse.

"Good Murad. You saw it on time." Rustam praised Murad loudly so that he could hear him.

"Yes, it is coming toward us," answered Murad anxiously.

"Hold on, be prepared for bumps and turns."

"Ok."

The jeep was going after them at a 30-degree angle; therefore, Rustam had a tiny chance to lose them even by driving faster. He stepped on the accelerator all the way and drove for a long time until losing the police jeep. And as soon as he entered the first village of the Almar District, he started going zigzag, making constantly right and left turns until he arrived at a narrow mud street with mud houses on both sides, where a car could not fit to drive. Rustam continued to the end of the street and then blew horn one time, and two times and then again one time, with one-second intervals between. An old looking metal door opened at the corner around the street. Rustam pulled his motorcycle inside, and the door got closed behind them.

"This is Haji Shahbaz, my cousin." Rustam introduced to Murad the middle-aged man, who greeted them and took them to a room through the back door of the garage. He offered to help with carrying the luggage that Rustam had just unloaded from the rack of his motorcycle. Rustam let him carry the luggage to the room where they all went.

"Who is this?" The host asked Rustam, pointing to Murad after he poured black tea to both of his guests.

"This is Murad, he is my future son-in-law, God willing," replied Rustam, unwaveringly, gazing at him as if Murad was already his real son- in law.

Murad did not show any reaction at Rustam's lie, but did talk to himself: "Why did he say that his daughter is not even ten years old yet? Besides, will this rich man give his daughter to a man like me who has nothing?"

"May God grant my older brother a stay in the heaven, he has a daughter about his age," Rustam said, pointing at Murad. "I am going to give her to him. He is a good young Muslim man, and always does his five times daily prayer."

"Thanks to God, we are Muslims, prayer is our religion, God granted this moral asset to us," said Shahbaz. "And thank God we are going to have such a good young man in our family." Shahbaz lowered his hands that he held up in the sign of prayer for thanking God, then asked his cousin. "Did you encounter any trouble on the way?"

"No, not much. One car was running after us, but I got rid of it."

"How, what did you do to it?"

"I lost it."

"Let me go, mess up the tracks of your tires in front of my house." Shahbaz got up and went out of his house quickly.

Rustam tapped Murad on the shoulder and told him, "Yes, Murad, you will be my son in law, I will give you my niece, God willing. She is a very good girl."

Murad still looked confused, as things seemed too good to be true to him.

"You know, Rustam Khan, that I am a poor man; have no money to pay you for the dowry or the wedding expenses."

"Son, don't worry about anything. I am with you; I will take care of everything, God willing."

Murad pulled himself closer to Rustam, who was sitting in a little distance next to him on a mattress, grabbed his right hand and kissed it. Rustam kissed Murad on the head in return. But he knew that now he could never ask Rustam shameful questions about his salary.

"I know you want to have your own money, and want to know how much your salary will be, right?" Rustam asked Murad as if he read his mind.

"No, Khan Sahib. It's all up to you, whatever amount you give me, I accept," said Murad with relief.

"I will be giving you 500 Afghanis every month. You will also receive a 200 Afghanis bonus every time we return from the trip of Almar. You will be living with me from now on as a member of my family, God willing."

"You are very kind Khan Sahib, may God make you more prosperous."

"Shahbaz Khan!" called Rustam to his host, getting up and going out of the room. Murad heard them discussing things in the next room, but did not know what they were talking about.

From the moment Rustam gave Murad a good answer regarding his salary, his mind had gotten occupied with another question as to exactly what kind of business Rustam was doing. He guessed he was doing *Teryak*- opium. He concluded it must be so, after thinking about the details of the Almar trip from the beginning, from the preparation of the trip, the luggage Khan carried and running away from the police jeep along the way.

He wondered if Rustam Khan was going to give him the 200 Afghanis after this trip to Almar. If he did, it seemed to him that he would be making a lot of money; he remembered Rustam saying they normally made two trips to Almar each month. With a quick calculation, he might be making 900 Afghanis every month without any expenses, which looked to him very much money in one month.

Becoming Rustam Khan's son-in-law still looked to him something incomprehensible though.

The next morning, Rustam and Murad ate a good breakfast with Shahbaz Khan and left for Andkhoy in bright daylight.

"You drive, son." Rustam handed the motorcycle key over to Murad. "Be relaxed; now we don't care about anyone along the way."

"Ok, Khan Sahib," Murad followed the instruction, as he too felt safe because he thought they were no longer carrying that dangerous stuff in that leather luggage at the back of the motorcycle. All he guessed was that they were now carrying a big bundle of money in in that luggage.

"We go home, not to castle; we need to get some rest tonight," Rustam said as they got closer to Andkhoy.

Murad's mind was occupied by the thoughts of his future wife all along the way. How old was she? Was she pretty? Where was she living now?"

At the house, Rustam's father hugged him warmly after Rustam announced to them his decision.

"Murad is a good Muslim an honest and hardworking young guy. And I decided to give him my niece, Dordana."

Murad got up and kissed Rustam's parents' hands. The old man and woman made brief complements about their granddaughter, who was staying in another room as she was not allowed to reveal her face to Murad or even to talk to him before their wedding.

"When do you want the wedding to be, Rustam? We want to see our granddaughter's wedding while we are still alive," said Rustam's mother.

"It will be soon, God willing after we come back from Almar next time," answered Rustam.

"Dordana's mother knows about her daughter's wedding or not?" asked Rustam's wife, who was sitting behind her mother-in-law with her face covered in a black veil.

"That is not important; she doesn't have to be let known. We make the decision," Rustam shouted.

Murad was happy to hear that Dordana's mother could not have a say on this matter. This way he would have one less person to worry about.

Rustam's wife silenced and never spoke a word again about this matter. She was covering her face from Murad at her husband's order now and forever because Murad was not related to her or Rustam by blood.

The next day, on the way to the castle, Rustam mentioned to Murad that he needed to learn how to fire a rifle and a pistol. Murad agreed. Likewise, Murad got familiar with other parts of Rustam's business that day. Rustam took him to a room in the back of the castle, where he was guided down to a basement.

"Here we make the powder from the material we receive," explained Rustam.

"Where do we buy the material from?" asked Murad. He was pretty sure by now that the powder was not something that was needed for making soap.

"We have brokers, they bring us the material from the South, like Farah and Helmand, and they charge us too much money, that's why I want to buy our own car, a Russian jeep to get things cheaper, God willing."

This time in the castle, Rustam took Murad directly to the drug processing room. Both men put on the required gloves, masks and gowns. Rustam gave one full-day training to Murad on how the little refinery worked. At the end of that week, they were able to produce enough material to fill the box, as Rustam called it. They put the product in plastic bags first, and then in the box- the old leather luggage Rustam carried every time he traveled to Almar.

"This time we can make good money, God willing," said Rustam as they started driving to their destination. And this time they did not come across a police patrol car.

Upon their return to Andkhoy, Rustam took Murad to the castle, to the factory and opened the box, which contained the bundles of 1000 Afghanis bills instead of the opium.

"Take, son, as much as you want," Rustam said to Murad, placing the money in front of him.

"No, Khan Sahib, you give me whatever amount you want to give me."

Rustam took some bills out of his vest pocket and handed Murad one brand new five hundred Afghanis bill and two one hundred bills over to Murad. Murad thanked Rustam and as a sign of high respect raised and kissed his boss's hand.

After this lucrative trip to Almar, Rustam decided that it was time to arrange Murad and his niece's wedding. He wanted to make this wedding merely a family event, and not to invite other relatives and friends to the occasion.

But Murad wanted to see his grandmother and his uncle invited to his wedding, hoping that this way he would be able to resume visiting their house time to time and keep family ties with them. Of course seeing Zarin was the prime goal.

Khan Sahib," Murad whispered humbly. "I miss my grandmother and my uncle; I want to see them at my wedding."

"Okay, I will go and invite Sakhidad and your grandmother, but you and I don't want to invite Ghulam, right?"

"Yes. I don't want to see Ghulam," Murad said resolutely.

"And you know that he will not allow Zarin to come, or even he will not allow her to reveal her face to you anymore."

Murad nodded angrily.

"You should no longer be thinking about your cousin as you are now getting married to my niece," Rustam warned Murad.

"Yes, Khan Sahib, I have forgotten about Zarin," Murad assured Rustam.

On a Thursday evening, a Mullah from the mosque in the neighborhood was invited to perform the *nikah*. Rustam and Sakhidad affixed their thumbs to the wedding contract as witnesses. For the purpose of the *nikah* to be performed according to Islamic sharia, Rustam acted as the authorized representative of the bride and Sakhidad acted as the authorized representative of the groom.

After the *Nikah*, Rustam gave 50 Afghanis and a plastic bag full of *Nuqul*-candies to the Mullah, who immediately was permitted to leave. The bride was brought into the room and was set down beside Murad, who was sitting on a wool-stuffed mattress covered with a green shawl. Dordana was also wrapped in a green shawl. The bride did not reveal her face to Murad until the time they went to their own bedroom. Apart from his mother and grandmother, it was the first time in his life that Murad had a woman sitting next to him. Now he had a woman at his side that was supposed to be going to bed with him tonight. "She is pleasurable as the flower of the heaven." He told himself, as he stole a glance at her face through the shawl.

Later in their bedroom, to him, she was the most beautiful creature in the whole world he had ever seen. He pulled up the shawl from her face. He gazed at her fleshy lips painted with a burgundy lipstick, seductively shining In the light of a kerosene lamp.

The next day Murad looked happy with his marriage, even though in the morning, the face of his bride looked a lot different from what he saw last night. After the morning wash, the wrinkles on her face made her look at least ten years older than him. He did not care.

Two months after his wedding, Murad accompanied Rustam to Farah province. There they purchased a used Russian jeep. The seller, a poppy grower by the name of Nazar Khan, trained both of them how to drive the jeep. Murad was a quick learner and was able to drive the car around in the city of Farah after two days of practice. Nazar Khan gave them a good deal in the purchase of raw *teriyak*– preprocessed opium as well.

It did not take Murad too long to learn driving on the clandestine routes between Farah and Faryab provinces. In their second trip to the south of the country, He even explained to Rustam the important turns along the way in order to avoid being spotted by a possible police patrol. Now by having such a smart driver such as Murad, Rustam's business got more profitable as he eliminated the middle-man who supplied them the raw opium.

"Where does Nazar Khan sell it?" Murad asked Rustam referring to the processed products.

"He takes it to Mashhad. Iran" answered Rustam hesitantly. "Maybe sometime in the future we will take it to Mashhad ourselves, God willing. What do you think?"

"Yes, Khan Sahib. But do you know how to go to Mashhad?"

"Yes. We can go through Herat province," Rustam said. "But we have to know the police commander of Herat because I heard that he is a very tough man, he wants a lot of money, or he will make us big trouble."

"Now we have our own jeep; we are not less than Nazar Khan.We can do it ourselves," said Murad with assurance.

"No. We should become partners with him from Almar to Mashhad because I don't want to lose him; he has a lot of connections there and can help us."

Rustam felt pleased to hear Murad talking boldly about his business.

One day Rustam and Murad happened to be driving by Sakhidad's teahouse, and Rustam suggested stopping by and eating a *chainaki*. Murad liked the idea. He wanted his uncle and especially Ghulam to see him driving a Russian jeep.

"Come, come! What a coincidence, It has been a long time we haven't seen each other," Sakhidad said, standing up to hug Rustam.

"Yes, brother Sakhidad, we are busy these days, could not come to enjoy your delicious *chainaki*."

"Good, good, Khan. You got a nice Russian jeep! How is my nephew driving it?" Sakhidad asked Rustam, extending his right hand toward Murad for kissing it.

"My son in law is a good driver," answered Rustam proudly.

"I was going to come to your house today or tomorrow to tell you the news. You know I have no telephone to call you."

"What news?" Both Rustam and Murad asked simultaneously.

"Your father sent me the news that you are being drafted into the military service," Sakhidad said turning to Murad.

"Oh brother, it's nothing. We can take care of that, God willing," Rustam said arrogantly.

On the way back home, Murad was silent. He was not sure as to where would he be sent by the government to do his service for two years, even though he did remember what Rustam had promised.

"Why are you so quite, son?" Rustam said and then tapped Murad on the shoulder. "We will be going to Maimana soon, God willing. You can visit your father and brothers and sister. Then we will see my other cousin Jalal Khan about your issue. He knows the police commander of Maimana. He is a very powerful man."

"Are you sure Khan Sahib I can be placed to Andkhoy to do my military service?"

"Inshallah-God willing. You shouldn't be worry because when I promise something, I do it even if it costs my life.

"Do you have to give them money to the police commander?" Murad inquired.

"Oh, yes. A lot of money maybe like five thousand."

"It's too much money Khan sahib." Murad's face turned pale.

"I will take care of it, God willing."

Two days later, Rustam and Murad left for Maimana in their Russian jeep. Their first stop was Murad's parental house, where they spent the first night.

"Thank God, I see my son after so many years, and he is now driving a Russian jeep," cried Murad's father, with his eyes full of tears as he directed them to the *Dalan-* living room of his old mud house. He looked tired and ill. Murad's brothers seemed grown-up men. Murad stepped out of the room to visit his sister and mother-in-law who stayed in a bedroom and were not allowed to come into the living room because of the presence of Rustam. His sister had also grown up into a pretty young girl.

The next morning, before leaving his parental house, Murad helped his brothers and sister with some money.

To his father, he said, "Don't give Fatima to a husband until I return from the military; I want to give her a glorious engagement party. Her future husband should be a rich man and must pay good money."

"Ok son, you are right. Her future husband should pay a larger amount of money," agreed his father.

The next day, Rustam took Murad to Jalal Khan's guesthouse in an upgraded area of Maimana, the capital city of Faryab province. Jalal Khan was a known merchant who was apparently doing the business of hand-made rugs between Afghanistan and Europe. But he and Rustam had been doing some partnership in Rustam's drug business. Jalal Khan had a close connection with the high authorities in Maimana, so he would always provide Rustam a protection from annoyance, usually caused by government employees.

Rustam introduced Murad to the Khan as his son-in-law and as his "right hand in the business."

"Is your boy a lion or a fox?" asked Jalal Khan earnestly.

"A lion, brother. He is a lion, and also, a loyal boy," replied Rustam proudly.

"Can he kill a fox?" Jalal looked at Murad.

"Khan Sahib, you just give me order, I will do anything you want," Murad said with confidence.

"Good, son, good. I am going to talk to the police commander to place you in Andkhoy for service. And be careful, never betray your father-in-law, okay? He is spending a large amount of money for you."

Murad nodded in the gesture of absolute obedience and quickly got up, kissed Khan's right hand first, and then kissed Rustam's right hand.

Rustam counted the five thousand cash and wrapped it back in a *Herati* handkerchief and placed it in front of his cousin.

Jalal Khan grabbed the money, took a note of Murad's full name, and then called the office of the provincial police commander for a private appointment. The appointment was made for the evening of the same day.

After returning from his meeting with the police commander, Jalal Khan announced to Rustam that Murad's placement as a police soldier in Andkhoy district was secured. Rustam and Murad returned to Andkhoy the next day with the proper paperwork in their hands, guaranteeing Murad's placement as a soldier in Andkhoy.

Murad was allotted to the post of reserve within the framework of the Andkhoy police station. Everyone in the town knew that anyone getting this post must be related to a high-ranking government official, a tribal leader or a rich man. Rustam was no less than any of these people; he had close connections both with the district governor and with the police commander of the district. Last month alone, after his latest trip to Almar, Rustam gave large cash gifts to both of them. Murad had witnessed this close connection each time he drove Rustam to the governor's and the commander's houses. Rustam always returned from such meetings with a big smile.

In his position as a reserve soldier, Murad was not required to report to the morning attendance every day or to perform the duty of patrolling the town in the night. Instead, he was allowed to go home in the nights, perform special summons, meaning to work as the special private messenger for the commander.

Murad was considering himself the luckiest person in the world; he was now a policeman. He had the power to arrest people, to do to them whatever he wanted, especially so because he was the private soldier of the highest police authority in the district. He was allowed to go home every night. He didn't have to perform the burdensome duties of minimum eight-hour street foot patrol or the duty of a night guard. More importantly, he was even able to attend to his business whenever Rustam asked him to.

But more than anyone else, Rustam was glad to see his protégé being inside the police force and thus, having eyes and ears within the office of the police commander. He could be now aware of what was going on in there, and who were coming in and out of the commander's office. He tried, during the first 3-4 months of Murad's service, to let him serve the commander as fully as possible, and did not use him much for working with him in his drug factory or in traveling to Almar more than once a month. In the meantime, Rustam would meet with the commander more frequently and present him cash or in-kind gifts each time. He did, however, order Murad to report to him about who commander's friends were and what was going on in his office daily.

As an insider, and as a confidante of the commander, Murad knew how much the commander loved money because Murad was the one and only person who would collect the money for him from every person who was brought into the office and was accused of committing a crime. Murad was getting smarter and smarter every day, and would always keep some money to himself. The commander knew that, and he was allowing it on purpose.

"Now is the time to give a good party to the commander in our house, God willing," Rustam told Murad.

After being a member of the police force for over six months, Murad was now called a *Konagi*- a veteran soldier. After his six months' probation period, he was considered experienced enough to be entitled to having more privileges, such as taking a day or two off within a month.

"Yes, Khan Sahib. He is very good to me." Murad agreed. "This coming Thursday night is a good time to invite him for dinner because next week he will be traveling to Kabul."

"Is he? What for? How do you know?"

"I don't know. This morning I was with his secretary when he came in and told him to make a report for him because he was going to go to Kabul next Saturday."

"Ok, this is a good time. And good you told me that," Rustam said.

On Tuesday, Rustam personally went to the office of the police commander and invited him for dinner for Thursday night, which was traditionally the time for getting friends and families together.

The commander accepted the invitation but asked Rustam, "What is the occasion, and who else is invited?"

"Sir, nobody else is invited as of now. This is just in your honor; If you like we can invite some of your friends or officers from your office too?"

"No. Keep it limited to us. I will come by myself. I am going to drive myself."

"Ok, sir. If you like I can come with my car and pick you up, and then take you back to your house?"

"No. I, myself want to drive."

On the night of the party, Murad was the one who washed everyone's hands in a portable aluminum sink and jug before and after the meal and also served the food. During dinner, the commander praised Murad's performance as an obedient soldier and as a good guy.

"Yes sir, he is a good boy. He is honest and you know he is a good Muslim too, he never misses his daily prayers," Rustam said, glancing at Murad with a gesture of appreciation.

After the food was consumed, Murad brought in a large bowl full of fresh fruits and placed a plate in front of everyone. After that he served tea to everyone, signaling the end of the party.

After sipping a little tea, Rustam cleared his throat and said:

"*Qomandan* sahib, with your permission, I want to ask for your kindness; Murad's father is ill, he wants to go to Maimana and visit him just for two days."

"He can go after I leave for Kabul, but make sure come back on Tuesday, okay?" said the police chief, turning to Murad.

"Yes sir, I will be back Tuesday," Murad replied cheerfully, jumping toward the chief and kissing his hand. "Sir, do you have any order for me? Do you want me to bring you anything from Maiman?"

"No son. Hopefully, your father is doing well."

"You are very kind sir."

"When will you be coming back, sir?" Rustam asked his guest.

"Maybe after one week," the commander said as he rose. He thanked Rustam and his father for the dinner and left in hurry.

"The guy that I talked to you about is our common enemy. Remember in Jalal Khan's house when he asked you if you could kill a fox? He was talking about this son of a bitch." Rustam explained to Murad right after the police chief left their house. "Last time the police from Maimana raided our factory and caused us a damage of thirty thousand Afghanis. Jalal Khan said that it was this guy who reported to the governor about us."

"We should do something about him then," Murad said with confidence.

"Yes, we need to finish him, God willing. If not, he is going to do a big harm to our business. Jalal Khan told me that he was in Maimana again lately, maybe he wanted to see the governor and say things to him about us again."

"So we need to do something sooner about him. We should do it before the commander returns from Kabul."

"You are right, son. After the commander leaves for Kabul, we have to do it in one or two days, God willing." Rustam said.

The noun fox stands for a very coward, illusory and deceitful person, that's why Jalal Khan and Rustam had been calling their common enemy, Salam Bi, a fox. He was from the Turkmen community of Andkhoy, involved in the same drug business as Rustam. He was presumed to be acting as the provincial governor's informant in the meantime, because of Jalal Khan, who was also a friend of the governor, saw him visiting the governor several times. So Jalal Khan and Rustam thought that all the troubles that happened to Rustam in the past were the work of this guy.

Therefore, the two cousins and partners wished to eliminate him.

The day after the commander left for Kabul, Rustam and Murad devised a plot to kill Salam Bi. They drove by his house, which was located on the eastern edge of Andkhoy, separated from it by a huge wasteland. They found out about the times of the evening that Salam Bi usually was going home.

It was a cold and cloudy Sunday night, a day after the police commander left Andkhoy. It was getting dark immediately after the sunset. Rustam stopped his Russian jeep two streets away from Salam Bi's house, behind a huge hill of rubble to pick up Murad after finishing the job. Murad, armed with a handgun and a fighting knife, walked back and forth in front of the target's house, waiting for him to arrive. The use of a handgun was reserved just in case the knife was not enough to do the job or the target fight back strongly. It was completely dark when Salam Bi returned home from his nightly prayer from a mosque about ten minutes' walk away from his home. Murad had wrapped his *shamla-* the loose end of his turban, around his chin and mouth, so he would not be recognized. He walked from the opposite side of his target and upon approaching him, he struck him in the stomach three times with a knife. Salam Bi, in his early fifties, did not get a chance to fight back or make a big noise for help. He fell to the ground and died on the spot.

Rustam was behind the wheel, his car's engine running. When he observed Murad running toward him, he extended his hand to the passenger- side door, opened it and put the jeep into gear.

"What happened?" Rustam asked Murad impatiently, pointing to him to get in quickly.

"I finished him, go Khan Sahib, go!" Murad shouted as soon as he got in the car. His right hand was bloody.

Rustam drove first on an unpaved road for an hour or so before they arrived at the main road in the district of Dawlat Abad. Murad cleaned his hand of blood, wrapped the bloody knife in a cloth that Rustam had had in the car for this purpose. Rustam made a stop when they arrived in a remote wasteland. He turned the headlights off and instructed Murad to take his bloody clothes off and put on the extra clothes that they had with them in the car. Rustam poured water on Murad's hands to wash out the blood. The weather was cold, but Murad did not care.

"When you go home, tell your father that you took two days off only to come and visit him and the family. He might ask you that how come you came in the middle of the night, tell him that your bus broke down on the way and it took the driver long time to fix it."

"Yes, Khan Sahib, I know."

The news of Salam Bi's murder spread in town and the province quickly. Despite the fact that at that time, not many houses had telephone lines, only high government officials, and a small number of very rich people, especially those who had a chance to visit a foreign country during their lifetime, owned rotary telephones in their offices or homes, this news spreaded rather quickly. The next morning, the local radio station based in Maimana, run by the government, broadcasted the news with no detail about the cause of the incidence except for saying that the cause of the murder might have been a family dispute. "The government will investigate the matter," the broadcast added.

A team of police led by the assistant commander of the district visited the crime scene but found no evidence. Salam Bi's body was not even taken to the local clinic, which was staffed by one doctor and one nurse, and did not have beds for patients nor did it have a freezer for keeping the corps. The team determined that Salam Bi was killed by a fighting knife. The investigation of family and friends who had gathered at the house had no idea about any suspect.

Salam Bi's body was buried Sunday evening, not only because of the fear that the body would decay in a couple of days but also according to Islamic Sharia, the dead should be put in the grave as soon as possible. There was a three-day *Fateha* held in the local mosque from morning to evening. During the *Fatiha,* relatives, friends, neighbors, acquaintance, and even some strangers attended the assembly, listening to the part of Quran recited by a Mullah or *Qari,* and praying for the dead, begging God to pardon his sins and grant him a stay in the heaven after the day of resurrection.

Rustam attended the *Fatiha* on Tuesday, the second day of assembly, and in a show of empathy to Salam Bi's family, he stayed in the prayer room of the mosque for a long time and prayed aloud to the dead each time at the end of the recital of the Quran. The mourning family appreciated the participation and staying longer during the *Fatiha,* as it was considered a sign of sharing their grief.

According to Rustam's instruction, Murad also got to the mosque right a few minutes before the end of the *Fatiha.* He said salaam to the attendants, sat down in a corner of the prayer room and prayed aloud to the soul of the dead with both of his hands up towards the sky. At the conclusion of the assembly, Rustam and Murad were among the few close friends who walked up to the family of the dead, who were standing up by the exit door of the room to say thank you to the participants. And they once again personally expressed their empathy to the mourners because of their loss and sent prayer to the soul of the dead.

On the way home, Rustam praised Murad for doing exactly what he had told him and getting back from Maimana on time and attending the *Fatiha* in its last minutes as planned.

"How was your father? And what did he said about your visit?"

"He was sick but was happy for my visit. I gave him and my brothers and sister some money," Murad said triumphantly. "He asked me how come I got there after midnight; I told him that the bus had broken down and it took a long time to be fixed."

"Good. Now that we are done with the fox, in a little time, I am going to appease the commander with a big gift so he would allow you to be free more days from the service."

"What are we going to do?"

"We will be making more trips to Almar," answered Rustam, trying to hide his excitement caused by the removal of his biggest rival in the area.

The police commander returned from the capital exactly one week after the killing of Salam Bi and immediately held a brief meeting with his staff in his headquarters. He got the full report of the incidence from his assistant who was the head of the investigation team and about the outcome of the investigation. As soon as he was done with meeting with his staff, he ran to the office of the district governor for meeting with him on this issue.

The commander summoned Murad when he came into his office the next morning.

"How was your father Murad?"

"He was very sick sir. He sent you his appreciation and his respect for letting me go home to check on him."

"What do you think about Salam Bi's killing?"

"I don't know sir, may God bless him. He was a good man."

"Go, son; make sure you bring me any news and information you get about this matter ok?"

"Ok, sir."

Murad reported to Rustam about the conversation he had with the commander. And Rustam called him again a "smart boy" and Murad also silently praised himself for planning things the way he had.

On the next Friday, Rustam really felt to celebrate the elimination of his enemy- Salam Bi- and in the meantime, give a treat to Murad for executing his orders in an ideal way.

"Murad, son, today I have a big appetite for Sakhidad's *chainaki*. Let's go and eat there," Rustam said as he got in the passenger seat of his jeep.

"Ok, Khan Sahib, I am hungry too for the *chainaki*." Murad smiled, feeling excited by the success he had in carrying out Rustam's orders, and also remembering that he was going to eat a whole *chainaki* by himself alone once again.

"You know, son? Life is too short, today you and I are going to do a *Nesha* together, ok?"

"What about my uncle, Sakhidad? He may be mad at me if I smoke hashish."

"You don't care about Sakhidad anymore; you are now a grown-up man."

When Murad stopped his Russian jeep in front of the teahouse, both Sakhidad and Ghulam gazed at it with jealousy.

"Welcome, Rustam Khan and Murad! You guys forgot about us, ha?" cried Sakhidad, getting up quickly, and hugging both of his guests. Ghulam also walked forward and shook hands with them.

"No, Sakhidad brother, we haven't forgotten about you, we are busy. The business of soap is getting hot. I am alone; Murad is busy with his service in the police force, except for some Fridays."

"Right, Murad son," said Sakhidad. "You are now in the police force, you should know about the killing, did they find Salam Bi's killer?"

"No uncle," Murad answered as if he was not much aware of the incident.

"How was he killed?"

"I don't know uncle. I was not here. I was in Maimana at the time."

"How were your brothers and sister?"

"They were good, but my father was sick."

"Brother Sakhidad, we are hungry, make four tasty *chainakees* for us," Rustam said, going to the back of the teahouse through the back door, and pointing to Murad to join him in the hashish- smoking party.

By completing the first year of his service, Murad earned more reputation as a loyal soldier and got more indulgence from his police chief. He got more freedom to go around in his civilian clothing rather than having to be in uniform. Every two to three months, he was allowed to be relieved from his service for two to three days, and comfortably worked with Rustam in the castle or traveled to Almar.

Rustam made his first trip abroad with the company of his cousin, Shahbaz Khan. He did so in order to establish foreign contacts and also familiarized himself with the nuts and bolts of the business outside the country. He visited a dealer in Mashhad, Iran, whom he had been dealing with in the past indirectly: now he met with him face to face so that he could train Murad. Having in mind more freedom for Murad and appreciating the favor done to him by the police commander, upon return from Mashhad, he purchased a children's bicycle for the commander's 12-year-old son.

The last six months of Murad's military service was full of valuable experiences; he made three arrests of the individuals that were, in one way or another, involved in the busyness of drugs. As a confident of the police chief, he was part of several nightly raids on the drug processing factories as well as on the drug transportation vehicles along the way from Andkhoy to Almar and Herat. He now knew who in his district was doing the busyness, what routes were used for drug transportation and even knew which drug dealers were out there walking free and had a connection with his police boss. On the order from his father-in-law, he reported to the police chief that the older son of Salam Bi was now running his deceased father's drug lab. He convinced his boss to give him three more policemen to search the suspected place. He destroyed the drug lab and arrested Salam Bi's son because he never "gifted anything to the police chief."

When the day of his discharge from the service arrived, Murad went to his boss's office, kissed his hand and after presenting to him a wrist watch, told him:

"Qomandan Sahib, this is a small gift for my brother, your dear son. I will be very grateful to you all my life as you were very kind to me. I am here to tell you that I will be at your service whenever you need me in the future." He used the exact words Rustam told him to.

Just two days after Murad got discharged from the service, Rustam's father died. Rustam and Murad got busy with the three days *Fateha*-praying for the soul of the dead. During the *Fatiha* several hundred Andkhoy residents including some of the high ranking government officials such as the district governor, the commander of police and the district attorney and many other dignitaries attended the prayer assembly. It was not only because Rustam's father was a reputable old man, respected by the community for his wealth and or being a good Muslim, but it was also because his son Rustam was the most powerful man in the town.

During the whole three days, Murad sat next to Rustam on a mattress as an indication that he was a member of the mourners' family. Other male family members, who were setting with Rustam, were Jalal Khan and Shahbaz Khan, Rustam's cousins who had come from Maimana and Almar solely for this purpose. The several hundred residents of Andkhoy, Sakhidad, and Ghulam among them, observed that Murad was an important member of Rustam Khan's family; because he was sitting on the mattress, among the group of the mourners, reserved for the close family members.

After the *Fateha* was over, Rustam and Murad rolled their sleeves up to produce a big box of powder for Murad's first trip abroad.

"This time you are going to Mashhad, God willing," Rustam said. "We should make good money in one or two trips because Eid-e Qurban is only two months away, I want to go to the pilgrimage to Mecca, God willing. You know the Hajj is the fifth tenet of our sacred religion, and every Muslim should go to the pilgrimage of God's house, the Holy Mecca."

"Yes, Khan Sahib," approved Murad. "Now that Haji Ba Ba, may God grant him a stay in heaven, is dead, you are our Haji Ba Ba. "Yes, son." Rustam tapped Murad on the shoulder.

Murad's first trip to Mashhad was a success. He first went to Almar and from there to Mashhad with the company of Shahbaz Khan. During their trip, Murad learned the nuts and bolts of the busyness, met with the connections in Mashhad and got acquainted with the culture of an International drug dealer. After the trip, he carried with him a letter to Rustam in which his cousin Shahbaz Khan praised Murad as a smart and a trustworthy boy. In his letter, Shahbaz Khan mentioned the count of the money that he sent to Rustam as his share of the profit. The amount was exact. Murad got good points, and from now on he became a real right hand to Rustam. He decided to go to Mecca without hesitation for his busyness or family; he delegated all his authority to Murad.

Before leaving for Hajj, Rustam announced his will to his mother, his wife and also Murad's wife, his employees in the castle and through them to his soap customers who owed him money. In his will Rustam informed everyone that in his absence, Murad would be his authorized representative, having the authority to run his business and supervise all his affairs. He instructed all of his family members to obey Murad when he was in the pilgrimage.

After returning from the Hajj, Rustam stayed home for one week to receive all the guests who came to congratulate him for performing the pilgrimage. There was more gray hair in Rustam's beard and mustache than were just two months ago. This change gave him more of a dignified look, and he was making gestures imitating his late father. Hundreds of family members, relatives, friends, neighbors, acquaintances, and friends, as well as many strangers paid a visit and demonstrated their respect to Rustam Khan for becoming haji. The seniors and the people of his age gave Haji Rustam Khan big hugs and kissed him on the cheeks three times along with using the high congratulatory words, but all others who were even a year younger than him, kissed his hands, and then rubbed their eyes and foreheads over both of his hands as they believed that these hands were now blessed because they had touched the *Hajar-ul-Aswad-* the holy Black Stone in Mecca.

Haji Rustam introduced Murad, who was sitting next to him all the time, to the visitors as his son-in-law and as a very good man. Murad would give away to each visitor a small teacup containing a sip of the

Zamzam- the holy water and a pair of *tasbeh* that Haji Rustam had brought from Mecca.

During the week-long ceremony of paying a visit to Haji Rustam's house, all the visitors realized that Murad was a dear and trusted to the Khan, and therefore, called him Murad Khan. Each time that he was called Khan, Murad deeply felt and enjoyed the pleasure of this title.

Murad Khan was now managing both of Haji Rustam Khan's businesses; the business of the soap factory and the business of "The Powder." He was distributing the products to customers and was collecting money from them. Unlike Rustam Khan, he could read and write a little bit and had the privilege to keep a written record of the business in the form of a pocket size notebook.

"I am happy to have a smart son like you," Haji Rustam said to Murad one day. He sounded ill. "We will be going to Maimana tomorrow to see a doctor, God willing."

"Yes, Haji Sahib, may God give you longer life, what is happening to you?"

"I don't know, son. I have a bad pain in the right side of my stomach."

"God forbid Haji Sahib, we should go to the doctor as soon as possible, God willing you will be fine soon."

But seeing doctors in Maimana and then in Kabul could not prevent Rustam from dying from his liver disease. After examining his blood, one doctor in Kabul told him, "It looks like you have been doing drugs for a long time."

"No sir, I have never done drugs," insisted Rustam.

"I don't know. Maybe this is the will of God, your liver is no good," the doctor said, leaving Rustam's room in the Ali Abad Hospital in Kabul. But Murad asked for a second opinion in the same hospital and then transferred his father in law to a more prestigious hospital in the capital- Avicenna Hospital. Here too, Rustam Khan's blood tests were disappointing, and Murad was told by doctors to take the patient home and accept the will of Allah. Murad was crying.

"Haji Sahib, I wish I could give the rest of my life to you! What am I am going to do if God forbid you are no longer with us?"

"Don't cry son, God is great, we accept whatever God wishes." Rustam tried to comfort Murad when they returned home and family gathered by Khan's bed.

According to Rustam's will, Murad Khan officially became the head of the family and the owner of both of his businesses. "After my death, my son in law, Murad Khan has the authority to take over the family affairs and to run my businesses, God willing." He groaned. "Murad Khan, take good care of my family, preserve my dignity and family reputation in the community, especially, safeguard my *namoos*," Rustam said taking short breaths.

"Yes Haji Ba Ba, your *namoos* is my *namoos*, I will treat your wife as my mother and take care of your daughters as my own sisters," Murad said while weeping.

"You, Jalal Khan and Shahbaz Khan, help Murad Khan in the businesses, and treat him like your own son."

"Yes brother, we will fulfill your wishes," both Jalal Khan and Shahbaz Khan stated dutifully.

"Don't give my daughters to beggars," Rustam whispered into Murad's ears.

Rustam's funeral event was the largest crowd that Murad had ever seen in his lifetime. He cried loudly when carrying Rustam's coffin over his shoulder from the mosque to the graveyard. The three-day *Fatiha* was held at the local mosque and Murad was the main male family member among the mourners accepting visitors' condolences.

After Rustam's death, Murad Khan maintained good family and business relations with both of Rustam's cousins, who were his partners. They conveyed Rustam's will to all of his business associates and customers that Murad Khan was now the boss of Rustam Khan's businesses. This helped Murad to guarantee his success in his daily affairs. Shahbaz Khan sent his twenty-year-old son to help Murad with his powder production operation, and also, as a family member, to take care of the family whenever Murad was traveling abroad.

Murad made foreign business trips mostly alone but never failed to get his partners' advice or to share with them the profits he was making fairly.

Murad Khan was mindful of the fact that for him to be able to control Rustam's family and be successful in running his risky business, he should act as strong as Rustam Khan did, both in his personal as well as in his business relations. He was especially watching Shahbaz Khan, who was a seasoned dealer and his only connection to the outside world. When Shahbaz Khan sent his son to help him in the business, he appreciated but also realized in the meantime that he should be careful and should always consider Shahbaz Khan's role in his affairs.

He trained Shahbaz Khan's son- Sohrab to drive the Russian jeep, and he would take Rustam Khan's seat whenever they were going to meet with dignitaries in Andkhoy or traveling to Almar.

As Rustam's two daughters were growing up, Murad was realizing the fact that the presence of Sohrab who was now living with them, might cause gossiping in and outside the family. Therefore, he devised a plan to kill two birds with one stone.

"Khan Sahib, may God grant Sohrab a longer life, he is a very good boy," said Murad to Shahbaz Khan during one of his trips to Almar.

"Yes, Murad Khan, "echoed Shahbaz Khan. "My son is a very smart kid."

"He is already a mature man, isn't it the time to tie his leg?"

"You are right Murad Khan. I was thinking about that too." Shahbaz Khan said in a tone of firm approval.

"May God grant him a stay in the heaven, Haji Rustam Khan's older daughter is fifteen already, and I can think of no better man for her than your son. I want to make Rustam Khan's soul happy by giving her daughter to one of our decent family members like your son."

Shahbaz Khan paused for a moment. "I like your idea," Shahbaz Khan said trying to hide his contentment at the idea. "I am going to come to Andkhoy next week, we will decide about the wedding arrangement."

In a week, the two men issued their verdict that Sohrab would marry Gulab, Rustam Khan's older daughter. The wedding arrangements took one month. A big wedding party was thrown in bride's house. Many high-ranking government officials including the district governor and the police commander, as well as other dignitaries and rich people, were invited.

"Performing Hajj is the fifth pillar of our sacred religion; every Muslim should go to the pilgrimage of God's home- the Holy Mecca." Murad Khan remembered Rustam Khan saying, and thought it was time for him to go to God's home and become Haji Murad Khan.

A couple of months before departing for Mecca, Murad Khan started changing his appearance. He let his beard grow longer. Started wearing white long *shalwar kamis* and a black turban made of *Paj* fabric, usually used by the semi-clergy men in Afghanistan and Iran; he would preach to Sohrab about the smart manner of doing business and dealing with the government officials.

"Whenever government people bother you, you take care of them by putting money into their mouth." He told Sohrab. "Maintaining good relations with the police people is particularly important because they can do anything to you; they can put you in every kind of trouble if you don't take care of them but they can rescue you from every kind of trouble if you make them happy."

Upon return from the Hajj, he stayed home for a full week and received the hundreds of people who came to congratulate him on the pilgrimage. He took the same seat in the large guest room of the house as Rustam Khan did after returning from Mecca, giving three hugs to those who were of his age or older than him and kissing on the head those who were younger than him. The visitors listened to him enthusiastically when he told them the stories of his pilgrimage to Mecca. He would also try to make short stories longer because staying at home for one week was boring. He could not wait to go out and take care of his business; he could not break, however the tradition of receiving visitors and staying home for one week, created by his father–in-law.

"I stayed in an expensive hotel near Kaaba and prayed Salaat five times a day in Kaaba by walking over to it. Thanks to Allah S.W.T, I was lucky to make my way in the crowd of more than two million pilgrims to put my hands on the *Hajarul-Aswad*- the Holy Black Stone. You know, there were thousands and thousands of people did not get the chance to reach it. Some fell on the ground, and some even died while struggling to reach the Holy Stone." Haji Murad said while demonstrating his hands. He also told the story of sacrificing a sheep, visiting Medina and performing the required ceremonies of traveling to Safa and Marwa and hitting the Satan by stones.

Life was going in accordance to Haji Murad Khan's wish. The business of powder was booming, the demand by the foreign customers was increasing. Shahbaz Khan advised him to shut down the soap business in order to dedicate all of his time and Sohrab's time to the business of powder. Sohrab proved to be a smart young man, and was capable of managing the operation of the drug factory and also able to control the family affairs while Haji Murad Khan was away, who lately had taken upon himself solely the traveling aspect of the business. He would travel to the district of Almar, and to the southern provinces of Farah and Helmand as well as to the western province of Herat to establish a larger network and make sure all parts of the operation are connected properly. Due to the magnitude of the operation, he alternated a couple of trips to Iran with Shahbaz Khan, who was until then solely responsible for the border crossing part of the operation.

As the bundles of cash they were making piled up, Shahbaz Khan proposed to Haji Murad Khan the building of a two-story building in downtown Maimana. This way, they could melt the cash they had in their houses on one hand, and make profits by renting the building to merchants, doctors and other businesses on the other. Haji Murad Khan agreed and quickly traveled to Maimana to meet with authorities there. Jalal Khan, who was also going to be part of the deal, facilitated achieving the permit for their investment.

It was April 27, 1978. Murad Khan was about to leave Jalal khan's house for Andkhoy when he was alerted by unusual and disturbing announcements made by Radio Kabul-Afghanistan. One declared the establishment of a Revolutionary Council; the other talked about the takeover of the government by the People's Democratic Party of Afghanistan (PDPA). The radio played the national anthem, national dance music and broadcasted the step-by-step progress made by the revolutionary forces.

"Khan Sahib," Murad said to Jalal Khan with an extreme anxiousness. "What is this? What's going on? I think things have gone bad!"

"Yes," Jalal Khan said speechlessly. "That son of the Russians did it."

"Who, who is the son of the Russians?"

"That teacher, son of a bitch," Jalal Khan said. His whole body was shivering. "I told the police commander several times to get rid of that *kafir*. He had nothing else to do but to do demonstrations on the streets and chant slogans against the government all the times."

"What are we going to do?" Murad asked.

"I don't know, Murad Khan. They are going to take everything from us, and they will even kill us."

"We cannot live in this country anymore," Murad whispered gloomily.

Both remained silent, listening to the radio, which was broadcasting the victorious developments of the upheaval. Jalal Khan turned off the radio, reached to his rotary telephone, which sat on a small table next to him. The telephone operator in the switchboard did not answer.

"I think they cut the telephone lines, the sons of *kafir*." He turned the radio back on; still, there were the same revolutionary slogans, and national dance music being played.

Murad's heart was pounding, he was anxious about his factory; about his car, about the hundreds of thousands of cash he had in his house.

But he did not have enough energy to move around during the whole long day of April 27th. He felt paralyzed and could not think of driving back to Andkhoy until it got dark. He left Jalal Khan's house after midnight.

"Be careful," Jalal Khan advised him. "Take the clandestine route, not the main route."

"Ok, Khan Sahib," Murad said, his hands shaking.

He drove very fast and got home when it was still dark. As usual, he blew his horn three times to have one of his family members open the gate for him, no matter what time of the day or night it was and no matter if the neighbors were still asleep, he would do so as a signal of his arrival. Once inside his house, he even did not reply to his wife's greeting and went straight to his bed.

"Don't open the door to anyone, I am going to sleep." He instructed his wife.

After a couple of hours of sleep, Murad woke up and tuned into the radio. The news was that the then President Mohammad Daoud was dead, that the revolutionary forces were in full control of the country. A declaration of the Interim Revolutionary Council threatened anyone "who commits sabotage would be dealt with categorically." He turned the radio off and decided to go out to see what was going on in the city. He thought of Sakhidad's teahouse, and suddenly felt a strong craving for a hashish smoke. He changed into relatively casual clothing, wrapped himself in a *dopata* and walked to his uncle's teahouse.

"Salaam, where is my uncle?" Murad asked Ghulam angrily, who was busy preparing the tea and the *chainaki* for the daily business.

"In the back." Ghulam pointed to the back door of the teahouse.

"Come Murad, smoke. Life is too short," Sakhidad said puffing out the dark smoke of the hashish hookah when he saw his nephew.

Murad rushed toward his uncle and hastily throw a kiss on his hand and then smoked a long round of the hashish hookah.

"What is going on uncle?" Murad asked, breathing fast.

"It's *pacha gardeshi*. A change of the king" Sakhidad answered, not sounding concerned about the events. "They want to bring in this country the same kind of government like the Russians' government. They will take the money and the properties from the rich and give them to the poor." Sakhidad spilled the events calmly.

Murad inhaled and then exhaled further puffs of the hashish as his anxiety augmented.

"What are we going to do uncle?" Murad asked nervously.

"I don't do anything. If they want to take my teahouse, so be it. *Luch az aab nametarsad.* A naked person is not afraid of water. I have nothing to lose."

Murad was silent, knocked down by the hashish. He felt like crying when the noise on the street broke the silence. Both Sakhidad and Murad sneaked out of the teahouse door.

"The revolution has just started; there will be no more feudalism and no more exploitation of the people. We will get rid of the oppressors, drug dealers and of those who got rich over the blood and the hard work of the oppressed," chanted one demonstrator.

"Long live the oppressed and the hard working people of Afghanistan. Death to the oppressors!" shouted another.

"From now on the poor and the hard working masses of Afghanistan will be the masters of the country, not the feudal, or the rich or the drug dealers," screamed a third demonstrator.

Ghulam joined the two sneaking out the teahouse. "God willing, from now on the government will take care of the poor and the working class. They are going to take everything from the rich and the drug dealers; I wish they do it as quickly as possible."

Murad felt a twist in his stomach; wished he could kill Ghulam right on the spot.

The demonstrators, comprising about two hundred or so people, mostly middle school students and their teachers and only a few ordinary people, made a stop in front of the teahouse. One of their leaders, a man in his early thirties, who was walking in the front row, came out of the crowd and turned his face to the rest of the demonstrators.

"Long Live the People's Democratic Party of Afghanistan!" He voiced as loudly as the whole bazaar could hear, throwing his right hand in the air. "Now we declare to all the enemies of the people of Afghanistan that your era has ended, now is the era for the hard working people and the intellectuals, the days of the reactionaries are numbered, now is the time for the progressives!"

He then turned toward the teahouse. "We will require the rich to explain to us that how they got rich, where did they get their money, their cars and their buildings from? And all of you listen, if anyone tries to sabotage the process of the revolution of the people of Afghanistan, we will crush you ruthlessly,"

"Who is this guy?" Sakhidad asked Ghulam. "Do you know him?"

"Yes, his name is Tufan, he is a teacher at the middle school. They say he is the leader of the party here." Ghulam answered.

Within a week, Haji Murad Khan's nightmare started coming true. He was detained by the new commander of the police; His drug operation stopped, his factory and his Russian jeep were seized.

"I know you very well," The teacher, the leader of the PDPA in Andkhoy interrogated Murad personally. "In the past, you were working in your uncle's teahouse, but now you are a rich man, you got rich over the blood of the poor. You need to tell me who are your partners in the drug business?"

Murad's silence was met with a hard kick in the stomach and a slap on the face.

"I inherited everything from my father-in-law Rustam Khan," Murad mumbled, trying to cover his face with his left arm from more slaps by Tufan.

"We are not blind, you stupid donkey! We know everything about you. You were just a teahouse worker with your uncle, but now you are Haji Murad Khan, you are a millionaire, Haji Murad Kha! Rustam was a drug dealer too. Now tell me who your partners are?" Tufan roared while hitting Murad harder kicks and slaps as he remained silent and refused to talk about his partners.

The next day, they searched his house and seized bundles of cash including Pakistani and US currencies.

Within two weeks from the day of the revolution, the new regime appointed new governmental leaders such as the provincial governor of Faryab and the district governor of Andkhoy. Tufan was appointed as the district governor of Andkhoy.

Within three more weeks there was countless news of harassments, arresting, and killing of the former government officials and of Khans, tribal leaders, merchants, and others who were considered by the new rulers as the enemies of the people of Afghanistan. Murad thought he was certainly on top of their list to be eliminated. He overheard the sounds of kicking, slapping, using slander by Tufan and other party members and new government officials addressed to other individuals who were detained and put in the adjacent rooms in the police headquarters.

He desperately needed help. He could not hope for Ghulam to help him but was wishing his uncle could do something for him.

The armed security guard unit at the police headquarter of Andkhoy was comprised of four members. Two of them were ordinary policemen, one with six months, the other one with one year service time; both were believed to be the ruling party supports and trusted to be at this job, at least for the timbering. The two others were young and inexperienced party members. One of the nonparty member policemen, the one with one year service time, knew Murad personally. He got acquainted with him when, the last time he and Rustam Khan visited Sakhidad's teashop, the soldier was there too as a customer. He knew that Murad had become Rustam Khan's heir and was now a reputable rich man. So the policeman countered him respectfully. One night when the young party members and his superiors were tired of daylong interrogations and beatings of people, and gone to sleep, Murad got a chance to talk to the acquainted.

"Can you help me, brother?" Murad said to the policeman.

"Cheshshsh, speak slowly Khan Sahib. What kind of help?"

"Just let my uncle, Sakhidad know that I need some money. Do you know him; he has a teahouse in the bazaar?"

"Yes, everyone knows him, one day I saw you and Haji Rustam Khan there."

"So you go to him tomorrow morning and tell him I need a 1,000 Afghanis. Please, may God bless you, and I will take care of you too."

"What if anyone knew that I helped you? They'd kill me."

"Submit yourself to Allah; there will be no one to know that you helped me."

"What are you going to do with the money? You cannot spend the money here; you are in jail?"

Murad went silent for a while. "God is compassionate; maybe someone will help me if I give him the money."

"How much would you give me if I help you?"

"All of them, 1000 Afghanis? I swear to God I will give you all."

"So what you need from me in exchange for the money?"

"You know, I have wife and family, they are in danger, I have to do something for them."

"So where would you go?"

"I want to go to Iran. I know people there; I can live there and work there."

"Can I go with you to Iran, and would help me there? I cannot serve these infidels."

"Yes, certainly God willing."

Three days after, Murad and the policeman crossed the border to Mashhad-Iran. There Murad found his opium business connections, and got financial support and was able to stay there for almost a year. He would meet with other people who were also crossing the border to Iran coming from different parts of Faryab out of fear or harassment by the new regime in Afghanistan.

During the next year, he received depressing news about his family: His younger brother and Sohrab were arrested; his mother in law died of heart attacks. He managed, however, to send the rest of his family to Pakistan because he planned for himself to go to that country where he could get training and prepare for jihad.

In 1979, following the religious revolution in Iran, Afghan refugees like Murad found a safe- haven in that country. Likewise, the training activities for Afghan warriors in Pakistan intensified. Haji Murad, still living in Iran, worked hard to organize a group of Afghan refugees to fight the communist regime in Afghanistan. He made a trip to Pakistan and received some military training, and then made a few clandestine trips to the vicinity of Andkhhoy and met with people in a couple of villages asking them to get ready for helping Mujahideen in the fight against the government. He also encouraged young villagers to go to Pakistan or Iran and train for Jihad.

On the night of December 24, 1979, Soviets tanks roared into Afghanistan under the pretext of protecting the country against "the invasion of American Imperialism". About the same time, Haji Murad was prepared to enter the southern part of his country from Pakistan and launch rocket attacks on the military targets there but was ordered by his superiors to delay the mission in order to devise a new military policy in the light of the Red Army invasion. He received a huge amount of arms and ammunitions along with logistics and cash and was ordered to set up a command post under his authority inside the country, preferably in the Northwest, where he was familiar with the culture as well as with the infrastructure of the area. He, of course, picked the Kalang village of Andkhoy where he knew from A to Z about it and where his drug processing factory used to be located.

He reported his choice to his leadership, it was approved, and he was titled the commander of Andkhoy. At the age of 35, he looked more mature than most people of his age. His slightly salt and pepper beard grew longer; he was now dressing longer white *shalwar kamis*, black turban and *Mazari chapan-* a colorful gown, usually put on by middle aged dignitaries. A made in USA shotgun was holstered under his shoulder, and a full bullet belt was fastened on his waist all the times.

At the start of the 1980s, the war against the Soviets and their backed government spread all over the country, from east to west, from north to south. Haji Murad proved to be a good warrior; he was able to mobilize people from around the Andkhoy district and launch deadly attacks on the government and military establishments.

From the day he was arrested and beaten and humiliated by Tufan, the former middle school teacher who had since been the District Governor of Andkhoy, Haji Murad never even a single day went to sleep and woke up without wishing to punish him. Therefore, stationing in Andkhoy and being in a position to go to war with that person and others like him was more a personal motive for Murad rather than a nationalistic or religious motive. He would personally take part in some of the night raids targeting the governor and his staff. But the PDPA member also tried to strengthen their grip on the power and tighten the security in and around the government establishments. Haji Murad became impatient with the condition and, in order to quickly kill Tufan, he could not but to devise a terror strategy. He designated a group of four Mujahedeen who had just arrived from Pakistan with fresh training in the field of hit and run tactics for his plan.

Commander Murad was extraordinarily mad when his younger brother's dead body was discovered in a wasteland outside the city of Andkhoy. The body was not recognizable at the beginning as it was covered by a mixture of blood and dirt. After Murad took his brother's body to a mosque and washed it, it appeared that he had been stoned to death. Murad thought it was the work of Tufan himself.

"I need you to kill the infidels inside the town, even go and attack them inside their homes and offices." He ordered the group. "You know? By killing any one of these infidels, you will become *Ghazi* and Allah promised you a permanent stay in heaven. Remember, the teachers," He paused, softened his throat and then continued: "Kill the teachers first! The teachers are the number one sinners because they are the ones who teach young sons of this country to become infidels, so killing one teacher is like killing five other infidels, don't spare anyone of them. You know, the biggest *Kafir* of all is the governor of the district who used to be a teacher, and who trained many *kafirs*, he is the biggest infidel."

Haji Murad's *Ghaza*–his terror campaign in Andkhoy, started with the killing of a middle school teacher who was walking home from the local mosque after the night prayer. Murad rewarded the killer by giving him a big hug and awarding him the title of his "friend."

When it was discovered later on that the teacher killed was not a member of the PDPA, Commander Murad said: "I don't care, they are all the same. If he were not a PDPA member today, he would have become a PDPA member someday."

Within two to three months, Murad's terror policy became a big issue in the district and the province. The teachers from the Andkhoy only middle school and a couple of elementary schools demonstrated several times in protest of the cold-blooded killings of the innocent teachers, but commander Haji Murad intensified his operation and thought of more organized ways of his jihad. He formed a group of five-hit people led by himself to operate in concert as such: Two people were assigned to the front line hit squad, armed with pistols to shoot the target, if one person fails, the second one will do the job, the two others, armed with machine guns hidden under their *dopatas*- traditional long clothes wrapped around their bodies, act as the backup hit squad in case the target itself or their security guards fight back. Murad, waiting in his new Russian jeep, would be watching the operation, and perform the final hit if needed. His new Russian jeep was provided to him lately by his "Green Eyed" friend as he would call his American advisor.

"Now you have a car with which you can drive around because it will be hard to distinguish it from other military cars operated by the government because it is painted the same color," said Murad's "Green Eyed" friend.

During almost four years that Murad was the chief jihadi leader in Andkhoy, he made several attempts to assassinate his big enemy, Tufan, the district governor, but except for one instance that Tufan was injured in a remote shooting on his car, the rest of his attempts were unsuccessful. Besides that, however, Murad was considered a tough and successful commander. Therefore, in the spring of 1984, he was promoted to the position of the Commander of the Northwestern zone. His promotion was followed by a reward by an Uzbek chieftain from Badghis province by offering him his 17-year-old daughter. This made Murad happy because now he got a family again in the area as his older wife and other family members were still living in Pakistan, and more importantly, he hoped that with having a younger wife, his wish for having a son would come true. From his first wife, Dordana, he had four girls but no son.

Murad wasted no time to bring his new wife home; He arranged a brief wedding ceremony in his command post attended by a total of six men including a mullah for performing the *nikah*-marital contract, bride's father, and uncle, Murad and two of his aids.

Murad loved Latifa. She was pretty and obedient. He would, sometimes, call her *Dokhtar*-e *Golabi*- rosy girl, as her soft lips and cheeks would turn red when being kissed by him and also whenever she worked hard cleaning the bedroom and washing dishes. His love to her intensified when she gave birth to their first son; when she brought a second son to the world, he was more proud of himself rather than Latifa as he believed that it was the indication of his strength that determines the gender of his product. In the past when a girl was born in his house, he would frown and say "It is God's will, what to say." If a girl were born in someone else's house, he would comment: "*Madah posht*"- loose-back, or feeble and feminine man, referring to the father of the newborn girl.

Commander Murad Khan's popularity spread beyond the national boundaries as the International Community, especially the United States got further involved in the military and financial support of the holy war. Murad Khan regarded by his American advisor as in asset and an important ally in the future of Afghanistan. Therefore, he would regularly and timely receive an adequate amount of arms and ammunition as well as a generous amount of US dollars.

When the rumors regarding the withdrawal of the Soviet troops from Afghanistan spread, Murad's American advisor reported to his boss that commander Murad Khan could be one of the valuable future leaders of the country.

"Khan Sahib," the advisor told Murad. "You can be one of the most efficient leaders of your country after the liberation."

"Thank you," answered Murad Khan with a hint of triumph. "When the time comes, I will need your help. I want to be the governor of Faryab."

"Ok, that's possible. I even think you deserve a higher job in the central government."

Finally, the time came, and in February 1989, the Russian troops left the country. Murad Khan expected that the leader of his party would become a major leader in the country and then he gets what he dreamt of, but it took at least four more years that the mujahideen came to power. During the four years of Dr. Najibullah's government, Murad Khan and his people made progress in occupying some parts of his district and succeeded capturing and killing about twenty local teachers and party members. Among the people he killed were Tufan's uncle and a 12-year-old nephew.

When Dr. Najib's government fell, and Mujahedeen came to power, Murad Khan was disappointed as his "Green Eyed" friend disappeared for good, and instead of becoming the governor of Faryab province, he was appointed the governor of the district of Andkhoy. He felt strongly that he should compensate his bad feelings with an achievement that would make heal his unsatisfied feelings. He summoned to his office one of his subordinates whom he had trained for Jihad and used to live close to him in Mashhad. Murad had seen the man's child, a ten-year-old girl, who was exceptionally pretty, and Murad had been dreaming all along to see that girl grow and become his wife.

"Samad," Murad addressed the man in a friendly tone. "I have seen you from the time of Jihad as a good Muslim and a good patriotic man.

I sometimes think that I should help you in making your life better" Murad paused. "How old is, Sheren, your daughter, now?

"*Wolaswal* Sahib," answered Samad, an originally Kabuly man in his 40s. "She is 20 years old."

"Do you know Samad, that it's a sin in our religion to keep a mature girl in your house and not to give her to a husband?"

Samad realized very quickly that it was the time for him to become a lucky man and to become Murad Khan's father-in-law. He was also certain if he refused Murad Khan's wish, his life would be in danger.

"*Wolaswal* sahib," said Samad humbly. "You were my mentor in jihad; now you are my big brother. You have a lot of rights over me and my family, my daughter is in your service, I accept whatever the tenet of our Islam says and whatever your order may be."

"God bless you, Samad, I knew you have a good heart," Murad straightened himself in his chair, extended his hand and shook the hand of his future father in law. "I want a quiet wedding, because you know I am so busy with the work of the government and other things."

"Yes *Woalswal* Sahib, I agree with you, and will do everything the way you like it."

The ceremony of *nikah* was performed in the presence of three people only; the mullah from the local mosque, Samad, and Murad himself. Murad welcomed his new wife in his freshly decorated bedroom the night after the *nikah*.

As the district governor of Andkhoy, the first thing Murad did was to revive his "powder" factory. He retook Rustam's castle, did some remodeling work to it, and built a large warehouse in it, where he stockpiled a lot of arms and ammunition that he inherited from the time of jihad. He instructed Sohrab and his younger brother who had just returned from Pakistan to reactivate the drug processing operation in full swing. Along with his new wife and Rustam's younger daughter, who was now 25 years old, he took residence in the official governor's residence. He told the rest of his family, his older wife Dordana, Middle wife Latifa, Sohrab and his wife and Rustam's wife to live in Rustam's old house.

"Daughter, you are here to help Sheren in daily things like sweeping the house, washing dishes," Murad instructed Rostam's daughter.

"Yes, Kahn sahib."

After six months of his governorship, he was invited by the governor of Faryab to a private dinner. He was already thinking of having a private meeting with the provincial governor, and now with his invitation, he thought of discussing his plans with his boss.

"Sheren," Murad Khan summoned his new wife. "Prepare my new coat and *chapan;* I am invited by *Wali* Sahi- the governor of the province."

"Ok, *Wolaswal* Sahib." Per his instruction, Murad was to be called *Wolaswal* sahib, Mr. District Governor, even by his wife and other immediate family members.

"Wrap one of the Kirmani silk rugs in a nice cloth; I am going to give it to *Wali* Sahib as a gift.

During his meeting with the provincial governor, a short fat man in his mid-50s, who was also a jihadi commander, Murad Khan listened to something that he did not expect.

"How are things going, *Wolaswal* Sahib?" The provincial governor asked.

"God is compassionate *Wali* Sahib; everything is going well," Murad replied triumphantly.

"You know, there are some ill-intentioned people here and there, they cannot tolerate seeing your success, and they are trying to destroy others' life," The governor whispered anxiously.

"Why should we care *Wali* Sahib as long as we are united?"

"You know *Wolaswal* Sahib, some negative things are happening these days," the governor got serious, he let a Marlboro 100 cigarette and added: "Wazir Sahib-e Dakhila- the minister of interior, called me the other day and mentioned to me that you were involved in things that are not consistent with the rules of our duties as public servants."

"Wali Sahib," Murad replied pulling his right hand over his salt and pepper beard.

"Wazir Sahib is a good-hearted man; he was my first commander when I first started the jihad. We should make him happy.

"Yes, we should do that or we will be in trouble."

As the result of their meeting, it was decided that the provincial governor travels to the capital and present a gift of a large amount of cash to the interior minister so that Murad and his provincial boss could safely continue their business.

The almost four-year era of the Mujahedeen government was in complete disarray; the seven Mujahedeen parties were fighting among themselves for power. Tribal fighting had spread all over the country. Especially, in the capital of Kabul, there were street fightings among the parties on the basis of tribal and language differences.

In this sort of situation, Murad Khan had a relatively calmer life in his territory. He had made a reliable alliance with the provincial governor, and with the district governors of the neighboring districts. Internally, he was resolute against any opposition; he would kill anyone on the spot who was disobeying his order as the district governor and would finish anyone who tried to jeopardize his drug business. Now there were two Russian jeeps and two American land cruisers with a total of a thousand private armed militiamen working under him. Besides, his operation was running from the southern provinces of Kandahar, Helmand, and Farah to the North of the country. After the collapse of the Soviet empire in early1990s, another foreign border- Turkmenistan opened for his business. Murad Khan became a full swing drug dealer plus a powerful ruler of the district of Andkhoy.

All of a sudden, a new movement by the name of Taliban appeared on the political scene of the country. The first group of the movement entered the southern province of Kandahar from Pakistan and took over all the southern provinces within months. After it took Kabul and toppled the government of the Mujahedeen, Murad Khan was smart enough to predict bad times for his business and his life. Still the district governor of Andkhoy, he made a secret trip to Iran for the purpose of strengthening his ties with his former contacts there and also deposited huge amounts of cash in his bank accounts in Mashhad. In the beginning of 1997 when the Taliban movement occupied most of the North of the country and was ready to take Faryab, he first joined the North Alliance in the fight against Taliban, but in the meantime, he relocated his three wives and their children to Mashhad-Iran. He then loaded his four vehicles with the remnants of arms and ammunitions for which he had already got the entry permit from the Iranian authorities.

During the nearly five years of the Taliban era, Murad was mostly busy with his drug business. Now that the Soviet empire had collapsed and Turkmenistan became an independent country, his operation was extended to that country. Crossing to Turkmenistan from the province of Faryab was extremely easy, and trafficking drug to Turkey and from there to Europe and America became a normal and smooth route for the business. He would, however, make clandestine trips to Punisher, where the headquarters of the North Alliance was located, and render his financial support to it in the anticipation that if someday the alliance returned to power, he will still have a place in it.

His calculation became true when following the 9/11, the United States' troops started bombing the Taliban. He hastily traveled to Pakistan and met with the leaders of the seven Mujahedeen parties, one after another, pledging his loyalty to each one of them. When in 2001, under the US air strikes, the Taliban regime toppled, and the Mujahedeen returned to Kabul, Murad safely went back to Iran and started moving his assets and family back to Faryab. In short period of time, a new government was in place in Kabul under the Bon Agreement, but the situation was far from normal as all the government institutions had been destroyed by the war. Administrative, legal and judicial establishments, the rule of law and public order did not exist at all. This kind of atmosphere provided an ideal condition for Murad to rebuild a drug processing factory, but this time a larger one, equipped with modern technology. By the time a new provincial governor, new police chief, and other high-ranking officials were introduced to Faryab, he was already known as the most powerful man in the province as he organized a group of over 1000 local militia under his command, armed with Kalashnikovs, shoulder-launched rockets and plenty of ammunition. Comparing to other warlords in Northern Afghanistan, Murad Khan was one of the most powerful.

The new provincial governor was his fellow Mujahid, whom he met in the early years of jihad while both were residing in Iran. They were trained together in Pakistan for attacking the Russian troop convoys.

The governor was from the Uzbek tribe. Murad also had told the governor that he also belonged to the same tribe. He introduced himself as a Pashtun to the leader of the Hizb-e Islami-e Afghanistan- the Islamic Party of Afghanistan, whose leader was a Pashtun, but called himself a Tajik when introducing himself to the Tajik leader of the North Alliance.

Murad Khan was often in the capital city of Maimana for having regular meetings with the governor; they participated together in the music and dance parties some Thursday nights. In all public events and official ceremonies whenever attended by the governor, Murad Khan would be seen beside him. Murad knew that in order for him to continue enjoying the freedom in doing his drug business and to be considered a dignitary, he would have to give a fair share of his drug benefits to the governor. The governor was also satisfied with what he was receiving from Murad.

Murad Khan was riding in his new Land cruiser, accompanied by two armed bodyguards. His driver was a trusted member of his militia. After the Jihad ended, he started wearing the three pieces suits, most of the times gray color suits, with white dress shirt and a red tie.

He started smoking American Marlboro100 cigarettes, imitating the governor of Farayab.

In 2005, for the first time in the history of the country, the law of election was past, according to which, local public organs such as provincial councils were created and publicly elected. Murad Khan lost his nightly sleep when he first heard this news.

"*Wali* Sahib," Murad Khan said to the governor. "I wish I were young so that I could nominate myself to the provincial council."

"You are better than tens of young people Murad Khan, go ahead nominate yourself."

"What if I don't win?" Murad Khan said sarcastically.

"No joking, Murad Khan," The governor said smilingly. "You will have no rival. According to the new law, there will be elections only a few months from now. You will be not only a member of the council but the elected chairman of the council."

"With your help, of course, God willing."

Murad Khan registered himself as a candidate for the people's representative to the council. He was encouraged by the governor to make some public appearances and make speeches. In Andkhoy, the only other candidate was a young, educated teacher. Murad knew that he could not have a good size audience for his speech rally in the town. Therefore, he planned to deliver a campaign speech in his local mosque, on a Friday after the Jumma Prayer, which is held in the mosques every Friday in the early afternoon, usually attended by large number of prayers.

Murad Khan was not a faithful mosque-goer, but after the first day of the announcement of his candidacy for the provincial council, he started going to his local mosque five times a day and every Friday for Jumma Prayer. This day, Murad Khan went to the mosque apparently for the prayer with a large number of his entourage, four of them armed with machine guns. After the prayer, the imam, who was aware of Murad's plan and was asked by him to make an announcement, immediately after the prayer, made a bold announcement regarding Murad Khan's speech.

"Dear brothers," announced the imam. "Now, our honorable brother, Haji Murad Khan, the well-known Jihadi commander, and famous Jihadi hero wants to talk to you.

All the players stayed and impatiently waited to hear Murad Khan.

Murad Khan was dressed like a typical Jihadi commander as posing for taking pictures: A black colored turban, white color *shalwar kamis*, a Pakistani Concealed carry vest, decorated with a holster full of the machine gun bullets.

"In the name of Allah, the compassionate, the merciful," Murad Khan addressed the crowd." "Dear people of Afghanistan, my Muslim brothers of Faryab, especially my dear countrymen of Andkhoy! You know I dedicated my entire life to the sacred cause of Jihad of Afghanistan against the Russian army. We all are Muslims, Thank God, you should vote for a Muslim and a Jihadi commander, not to the infidels, like teachers who disseminate anti- Islamic ideas.

"Allah-o Akbar, God is great!" shouted the audience initiated by Murad Khan's entourage.

"Long live the Great Mujahid, Haji Murad Khan!" The crowd added.

"If you vote for me, I am sure God will bless you and render you a stay in heaven. Also, I will serve you and take care of you. Whenever you have a need for anything, money or otherwise, I will be here to help you," Murad Khan concluded his speech.

At the end, Murad Khan's entourage handed over an envelope containing two hundred Pakistani rupees to each one of the attendants.

As the first ever elections in the country were held, the people of Andkhoy elected Murad Khan as their representative to the provincial council.

The governor of Faryab congratulated Murad Khan over the phone and invited him to his house one day before the provincial council convened its first opening session and picked its chairman.

Murad Khan, triumphant for his election to the provincial council, but still in need of the governor's help for becoming the chairman of the council, hastily handed over a gift wrapped in a new Herati handkerchief to the provincial governor as soon as he entered the residence of the governor. The governor gazed at the gift, gave a big hug to Murad Khan, and then unwrapped the gift as he took his seat at the leather swinging recliner. He invited Murad Khan to take a seat next to him.

"May God grant you a longer life Murad Khan, there was no need to bring me this."

"It's nothing Mr. Governor, I have a lot of respect for you, and without your help, I could not be elected to the council. I will do more for you whenever you ask me to."

"Thank God who gave me such a good friend like you," The governor said as he completed counting the bundle of ten thousand US dollars. "Your election to the position of the chairman of the provincial council is guaranteed, I have so much influence over many of the elected council members that I can make happen what I am saying."

Only a few days later, Murad Khan celebrated his victory as the chairman of the Faryab provincial council by inviting the governor and some of his friends to Maimana Hotel. Among the guests were almost all and every government high ranking official of the province, most of whom were Murad's former fellow Mujahedeen commanders, some parliament members who were in Faryab for vacation, as well as a good number of local tribal leaders and rich merchants.

CHAPTER 2

SHEAR ZAMAN TUFAN

It was the last day of June. The air was pleasant and aromatic on a breezy afternoon in Kabul. Today was one of those rare days that there were no sounds of bullets or rockets being fired in different parts of the city, nor the news of any suicidal attack was heard in the vicinity of the Taimany area. Tamana was watching the blue sky through the window of her room on the second floor of her house, and then examining her cellular phone, again and again, expecting a call back from Samim. She would repeat calling him every 10-15 minutes, only to be disappointed by seeing the number of her calls being increased each time. She then called her cousin Hakim, who was a close friend of Samim, but he neither had any idea about Samim's whereabouts.

Today, one of the best dreams of her lifetime had come true. She could not wait to share her excitement with her loved one. "Thank God Tamana graduated from high school, thank God Tamana graduated from high school!" She was singing while looking at the sky, and imagining herself in a white wedding gown along with Samim in a black suit, red bow on a white suit shirt, hand to hand, standing side by side by the exit door of the Kabul Hotel, saying goodbye to the guests at the end of their wedding party. She knew that the realization of her second dream was depending on her father's consent, without which she would not be able to get married with the love of her life, Samim. As of that moment, she hadn't even revealed to her mother her secret of loving Samim, even though her mother was very kind to her. Her anxiety got increased by every minute because she did not hear from him the whole day, therefore decided to talk to her mother about it so that she could openly search for him.

"Mother," She sat next to her on the sofa in their large living room. "I need your help,"

"What kind of help daughter?"

"Now that I graduated from high school, I have another dream."

"Of course, I will help you like always. I know you want to go to university and become an engineer, right?"

"Yes, mother, but there is something else."

"What is that, tell me? I am going to help you with anything you want; you are my only child."

"I like someone," Tamana said putting her head down.

"Who is that someone daughter? Tell me," Tamana's mother said while rubbing her daughter's right hand with hers.

"I know, Ba Ba is not going to like him, but he is a very good boy."

"Who is it? Tell me."

"Samim, Murad Khan's son."

"Oh, no daughter, your father will be mad if he hears this."

"I know mother, but I need your help,"

Tamana's mother said anxiously. "I am not sure if he will listen to me. Your father and Murad Khan are historic enemies; they are thirsty to each other's blood."

"Samim and I both know that, but we don't care about their hostility. Samim is not like his father."

"Ok, I will try to tell him someday when he is in a good mode; nowadays he is very busy with his construction business."

Tamana put herself in her mother's arms; her mother combed her hair with her fingers for a long while.

In the night, Tamana went to bed earlier out of fear of her father and let her mom talk to him one on one. But she could not sleep until her father came home, late as usual. Her mother stayed awake until her husband ate his dinner and got relaxed, then started talking to him. Tamana was listening to the conversation and overheard her father raised his voice as expected.

The next day, while Tamana was still in her bed, his father kicked her on the legs and ordered her to wake up and talk to him.

"This was not what I was expecting from my daughter," Shear Zaman said angrily. "I sent you to school to get high education and then bring to my home a decent boy whom I could call my son, but you are bringing home the son of my enemy!" Shear Zaman said standing by his daughter's bed, not even giving her to get up."

"He is a good boy dad, he is not a criminal," Tamana said humbly.

"I don't like this son of a donkey. Are you aware or not that Murad is a criminal, he killed your uncle and so many other innocent people, his hands are stained with the blood of tens of children and women? I don't want to hear about him from you anymore, or I am going to kill hi!"

"They are young and educated, they like each other," Tamana's mother intervened as she came into the room. "The boy has been living in Kabul for a while; maybe he is different from his father."

"You shut up, how do you guarantee that the son of a barbaric wolf could be something other than the wolf?"

"He says both of us should go to university and become engineers, then make a nice family. He doesn't like his father," Tamana said while weeping.

"I don't want to hear this anymore, this is my rule, and nobody can break it." Shear Zaman said loudly, leaving the house.

Shear Zaman was born in the Malistan district of the Ghazni province, bordering the capital city of Kabul. His father, who had a middle-school education, was a teacher at the elementary school in the district. As the first child of his parents, Shear Zaman was well cared for, especially his mother would call him *jigaram*–my dear. When he was ten, his father's younger brother was killed in a street fight. When the wounded body of his uncle was brought home, his face was covered with blood and dirt. It was unrecognizable and scary. Shear had nightmares for weeks and could not sleep. His uncle died two days after the injuries, but his father could not afford to take him for treatment to a hospital in Kabul.

Later, Shear understood how his father spoke of the incident. "My brother was brutally stoned to death by the thugs of Zarif Khan's son."

"Why didn't the government go after the killer?" Shear's mother would ask her husband.

"Who is the government? The district governor is afraid of the Khan. Nobody can arrest Khan's son. Khan has money, drug money. The provincial governor is his best friend." Shear's father said while his tears were running down his short pepper and salt beard.

By listening to the story of his uncle's death over and over again, Shear Zaman developed a fierce feeling of hate against the Khan, who was a drug smuggler and the most powerful man in the district. Shear Zaman and his brother, Shear Alam, a year younger than him, constantly dreamt of revenge against the Khan.

Shear's father was one of the handful people in the district who enrolled his two sons in the elementary school and then sent them to high school despite the opposition of his wife, who wished their sons be sent to the local mosque for religious studies instead. After graduating from high school, both brothers started their first career as teachers at two different middle schools in Ghazni, the capital city of Ghazni province. The two brothers rented a room in a travelers lodge, located halfway to the schools where they were teaching.

After two years on the job, the two Shears became known to the authorities as dangerous people and decided to remove them from the area. Shear Zaman was sent to the Middle School of Andkhoy District, and Shear Alam was sent to the Middle School of Almar District as teachers. The two were sent to these Uzbek-dominant districts because they belonged to the Tajik tribe, and historically the two tribes were not in good terms with each other, especially in those areas. Thus, the authorities in the Education Ministry hoped that this way the two brothers will not be able to influence the local teachers and students there, and further hoped that they would be isolated. But the two brothers called their appointment to these districts as an exile and vowed to continue their revolutionary activities regardless of what was going to happen to them.

In the early 1970s, the two brothers became members of the People's Democratic Party of Afghanistan, a leftist party. Along with that, both brothers choose for themselves the last name of *Tufan*, meaning storm.

They were actively involved in attracting other teachers and students to the ranks of their party, organizing street demonstrations against the government and disseminating Marxist-Leninist ideas.

In the after school hours and on Fridays, Shear Zaman Tufan would go to a downtown restaurant in Andkhoy and get together with other teachers and individuals who were interested in politics. These gatherings were called *Gardab,* meaning whirlpool. *Gardab* was the place for discussing politics and making arguments among opposing opinions. These arguments would sometimes become very heated and even escalate to a physical fight, especially between Shear Zaman and those teachers who advocated Mao Zedong's ideology or the ideology of Islamic brotherhood. These politicians accused one another of being traitors and foreign agents.

More than anyone else, Shear Zaman claimed to be a true friend of the poor and tried to make friends with individuals from the working class.

"Great Lenin called the people of working class as the proletariats, and proletariats are the true revolutionaries," Shear Zaman mentioned to his comrades time and again. "Our tea server can be one day a vanguard revolutionary," he added, referring to the person who was working as a waiter at the restaurant where *gardabs* were convened. Whenever he went to the restaurant, Tufan shook hand with the servant and tried to have a word with him.

"Where do you come from?" He asked the server.

"I am from Ghore province."

"How come, you came here for work; you couldn't find a job in Ghore?"

"No sir, there was no job in Ghore."

"Whom do you live with here?"

"We are five workers living in one room there," the server pointed to a mud-walled room on the top of a shoe- repair shop across from the restaurant.

"Do you have children?"

"Yes. Two girls, one boy."

Shear Zaman showed sympathy to him. He was having an eye on the young worker to bring him into his party ranks, and thus, earn credit among his comrades for so doing.

"How much they pay you here?"

"100 Afghanis a week,"

"How many days do you work?"

"Every day, seven days a week, from early morning to the night," the server explained.

"This is not fair; this is exploitation!" Shear Zaman screamed. "You know, you work very hard and work too much, but they pay you very little. They make money out of your hard work. This should be changed, that's what we- the members of the People's Democratic Party are trying to do. We are trying to bring about a fair and just system, where the people like you will get paid enough to feed their families. I know you don't have your own home in Ghore, do you?"

"No, sir. My wife and my children live in a basement with the owner of the house; we pay rent."

"All four of them live in one room? And I am sure your wife works for the homeowner, right?"

"Yes, Tufan sahib, you are right."

After speaking with the waiter for almost two months, Shear Zaman announced to his party committee at its weekly meeting that "Comrades, I am proud to inform you that I will soon bring to the ranks of our party a worker, a restaurant server who is going to be a true revolutionary in the future."

"Long live Comrade Tufan, you are doing a historic job!" The rest of the committee complimented him.

Qambar Ali, a 28-year-old man from *Hazara* tribe, had been working in the restaurant for ten months and so far had saved one thousand Afghanis from his salary. One day he told Shear Zaman that he was planning to go home and visit his family next week. He said he would be back in two weeks.

"Ok, comrade, I wish you a good trip home, come back soon, we will need you here for some important things," Shear Zaman instructed the server calling him already comrade.

"Ok Tufan sahib, but what kind of important things you need me for?" said the server while taking his wallet out of his pocket to show the pictures of his children to him. Shear Zaman looked at the picture showing all three of Qambar Ali's children, and in the meantime, saw the bundle of the hundred Afghanis bills inside the wallet.

The *gardab* was getting hotter and hotter by the passage of every day. Tufan and one of his former students and a young party member, named of Afzal whom Tufan called "A revolutionary young boy" tried never to miss the *gardab*. But as time went by and the PDPA ranks were expanding inside the school, where he was teaching, Tufan got caught up in the party affairs most days after work hours and missed the *gardab*. But his favorite young comrade, Afzal was obligated to fill for him at the *gardab*.

The next Friday, as soon as Shear Zaman and his companion entered the restaurant and took their seats at the usual corner, Qambar Ali ran to them crying, "Tufan sahib, for God sake I lost my money, my wallet, what should I do? I was going to go home next week." The server had tears running down his cheeks.

"How, and where?" Shear Zaman asked in a sympathetic tone.

"Here, inside the restaurant."

"How do you know, you lost it inside the restaurant?"

"Because I remember I had it with me yesterday morning, but in the night I did not have it."

"If it's lost, it's lost. You are not going to cry, you are a grown up man, and you are going to be a revolutionary, you should not cry after money."

"What? A revolutionary man shouldn't cry? That was my children's money. I was going to buy them clothes, oh God! What should I do?" He turned away from Shear Zaman.

Shear Zaman and Afzal, one of his young comrades, were tired that day from having very lengthy and heated arguments with their ideological opponents. Shear Zaman was also a bit disappointed with Qambar Ali who cried for money and unlike before, was not in a mood to listen to his lecture. Tufan shared his frustration with Afzal and asked him not to give Qambar Ali a serious consideration from now on.

"Comrade Tufan," said Afzal while both leaving the restaurant after the *gardab*. "Yesterday, when I came to the restaurant and was going to use the bathroom, I found a wallet on the floor. I looked inside; it was Qambar Ali's. There were a 1000 Afghanis in it. First I thought I should give it back to him, but I said to myself that I should wait to talk to you about it first and to get your advice whether I should give it to him or not, so what do you think dear comrade?"

"Thank you, comrade, for not giving it back to him; we should not do that, do you know why?"

"No, please you tell me, dear comrade. I will do whatever you suggest."

"There is a good and logical reason behind this: You are the servant of the people, you make a sacrifice for the good of the masses of the oppressed people and feel for their sufferings. Therefore, you have the right to make a decision for their good. If you don't give him the money, he will become more of a revolutionary man. He will get more hard feelings toward his exploiter, the restaurant owner who pays him such an unfair wages, thus he will be more ready to become a real revolutionary man and decisively struggle for the cause of the people," Shear Zaman lectured his young comrade as they were walking to their homes. "And furthermore, as a dedicated son of the people, you have many rights over the people."

"As always, I really admire your logical reasoning and the way you analyze matters. I completely agree with you but would like to respectfully request you to please accept half of the money because, no doubt, you are also the true son of the people and make a sacrifice for the good of the oppressed people many times more than I do. So please accept!"

"In my opinion, the money is yours because you found it, but since you insist, I will accept it for the sake of my personal feelings toward you as my dear friend and comrade." Shear Zaman, said grabbing the 500 Afghanis from his friend's hand and putting it in his pocket.

The times of Murad Khan's business boom and the escalation of the revolutionary movement in the country had coincided. As in many areas of the country, there was a strike or a demonstration on the middle school campus or the streets of downtown Andkhoy and Almar almost every week.

Ever since the two Tufans were appointed as teachers in the middle schools of Andkhoy and Almar, Murad Khan was constantly bothered by a noise on the streets of the two districts. He would hear the slogans of "Death to the oppressors, death to the exploiters and bloodsuckers of the people of Afghanistan and death to the drug smugglers," time and again.

Murad Khan and other dignitaries complained several times to the authorities about these activities and call the two brothers infidels and even considered them followers of the Russians' ideology. The two brothers were summoned to the district governor's offices a few times and were warned about their activities as a danger to the national security. But the two would strongly argue with the district governors and even call them the supporters of the enemies of the people of Afghanistan.

One time the district governor oof Andkhoy made Murad Khan and Shear Zaman met face to face in his office. The district governor arranged this meeting in consultation with Murad Khan for a purpose.

"Tufan Sahib, I invited you to this meeting to talk to you about an opportunity for you," the district governor said. He paused for a relatively longer while, waiting for Murad Khan to join the meeting. "I think you are a talented and smart person and deserve a higher place in the education system so that you can be of more help and service to our children," he added.

When Murad arrived, the district governor introduced his guests to each other.

"This is Mr. Tufan, one of our best teachers in the district, and this is Murad Khan our friend and a decent man in the district."

"Yes, I know him, who doesn't know him? He is a popular person," said Murad assertively.

"Thank you," Shear Zaman Tufan said.

The governor continued talking to Tufan. "As I said, you deserve to be in a higher position in our education system. I thought I should propose to the governor of Faryab and through him to the Ministry of Education to appoint you as the education director of the district."

"I support your idea *Wolaswal* Sahib," Murad Khan said, putting *Naswar*, a mixture of minced tobacco and limestone, in his mouth. "Tufan Sahib should be appointed as the education director of the district."

"Thank you both, I am a servant of the people, and will do anything I can do to serve the students." Tufan seemed astonished by the nature of the meeting.

"In the meantime, we want you to put an end to things that are not good for our children and our country," the district governor said, gazing at Murad Khan instead of Tufan.

"*Wolaswal* Sahib is right," Murad said. "You know, these are the things that God doesn't like them, and the people don't like them."

"What are you talking about? What is that I am doing and is not good for our country?"

"We are talking about taking the small students to the streets every day, wasting your time and their time and accomplishing nothing," The district governor said.

"I will give you some money as a gift so you can buy some good clothes and other things for yourself; just abandon these useless things like screaming on the streets. All the people laugh at you anytime you do this thing." Murad Khan said.

"You are wrong Murad; your money is drug money. I am not a beggar. I don't want your charity. You cannot stop the storm of revolution by your money or position." Shear Zaman said and got up to leave.

"You are the follower of the Russians; you will be put in hell by God." Murad Khan spat at the teacher.

"Someday, you will pay for this, you traitor," Tufan shouted, slamming the door behind him.

The next day, Tufan was detained and charged with the sabotage of national security. He was put in the basement, called the detention center of the district governor, located right underneath his office. He was interrogated, beaten and humiliated by the district governor himself.

After spending less than a week in the detention center, Shear Zaman was released by his comrades. The next day he celebrated the victory of "The People's Revolution" on April 29th, 1978 by launching a large demonstration in downtown Andkhoy. He mobilized and took to the street a crowd of around 200 people, mostly school children and teachers and some ordinary people. He was walking at the front of the demonstration chanting the slogans such as "Long live the revolution of the hard working people of Afghanistan," "Long live the Party of the People Democratic Party of Afghanistan," and "Death to the counter-revolutionaries, the exploiters, and the drug smugglers."

Listening to these slogans, Murad Khan, who was hiding in Sakhidad's tea house, realized that his days were numbered if he did not go away as soon as possible.

With the help of his uncle, he managed to escape to Iran. But his brothers Allahdad and Sohrab were too occupied with the lucrative business of "powder" and ignored all the warnings and advice coming from Murad Khan to leave the country as soon as possible. In the very first month of the upheaval, they decided to make another drug smuggling trip to Almar instead. This time again, they made a tremendous amount of cash and were lucky to avoid any trouble on the way back home. But at the gate of their castle, they were met by three armed persons from the new security force led by a PDPA member. All three were dressed in civilian clothes, but carrying Kalashnikov machine guns under their garments. Both were beaten with the bottom of the Kalashnikovs until they passed out. Per instruction from Shear Zaman, who was appointed the district governor of Andkhoy on the third day of the "April Revolution," Murad Khan's brother was separated from Sohrab and was taken to the same basement where Tufan was once put in by the then district governor, located right under the governmental structure.

"Ok, you son of a donkey," shouted Shear Zaman Tufan, entering the basement alone, and kicking Allahdad on his big belly, causing his cuffs and chains to make sounds. "Now you are in the hands of the people's revelation; you have to pay the price for all the people's blood that you and your brother have sucked during the years."

"What? What did I do, Tufan Sahib? For God's sake *Wolaswal* Sahib, I can share with you whatever money I have made from my work," whispered Allahdad, wheezing loudly.

"Ha, ha!" Shear Zaman threw a couple of hard blows to his captive's head and face with his heavy boots. "Where is Murad, your brother?"

"I don't know; I haven't talked to him this whole week."

"Liar, you son of a liar, I will kill you if you don't tell me where he is," Shear Zaman roared, throwing three more blows to Allahdad's bloody face and chest.

"He left for Iran," Allahdad said in a very low voice trying to avoid swallowing the blood running down from his nose.

When back to his office, Shear Zaman asked his security guard to leave him alone. He opened the briefcase that he'd confiscated from Allahdad, and examined the cash in it.

"So much American dollars, these traitors are doing international drug trade," he whispered to himself.

After hiding the money in the drawers of his office desk, Shear Zaman convened a meeting of his party and government leadership, comprising the new party secretary, who was chosen by him, the new police commander, the attorney general and the intelligence chief.

"Dear comrades," Shear Zaman Tufan addressed the meeting. "As you all are aware, today we have one of the biggest enemies of the people of Afghanistan in our hands, but unfortunately, we were not able to catch his brother Murad who is an even bigger enemy of the people. I want all comrades to go out and look for him, day and night. I want him alive unless he tries to shoot you. As far as Allahdad, we all know that he is also a big bloodsucker and exploiter and therefore, should be punished severely. Our meeting here is functioning as the special revolutionary court and can issue its verdict. I propose that this enemy of the people of Afghanistan should be executed."

The verdict was approved unanimously by the meeting. Shear Zaman asked his comrades to give him the honor of taking care of this big enemy of the people by himself.

His request was granted with applause.

The manner of executing Murad's brother was the subject of Shear Zaman's thoughts for a couple of days, and when he came up with an idea, he ordered his security staff to carry a load of stones and a duct tape down to the basement. On the day of execution, he put on his jeans, a woolen sweater, and high boots.

Allahdad was already cuffed and chained. Tufan taped his prisoner's mouth and then started hitting him with the stones, weighing about a kilogram each. Allahdad was weeping, screaming soundlessly, turning and tossing until passed out. Shear Zaman would take a break after throwing 10-12 stones at his enemy and then start throwing the rocks again, while uttering the same words: "You son of a donkey, you oppressor, you traitor, the enemy of the people of Afghanistan." At the end, he took a deep breath, satisfied with fulfilling his "sacred" duty.

According to the verdict of the revolutionary court, Allahdad's dead body was not given to his family; it was tossed in a remote area of the district's deserted area instead.

As the executive leader of the district, Shear Zaman considered his first and foremost revolutionary obligation to finish the enemies of the people before doing anything else. He delegated many of his administrative responsibilities to Afzal, who was now 22. Afzal was the son of a blacksmith, and therefore Tufan would consider him a" true revolutionary" and gave him the title of "Legendary Revolutionary Boy,". Shear Zaman had had him in mind for a leadership post in the future from the very beginning of their acquaintance. In the meantime, Afzal was fully loyal to Tufan and would always praise him as his mentor for his able leadership.

In his list of the enemies were included three teachers who had been teaching at the same middle school as Shear did. Some of them had different ideas regarding serving the people of Afghanistan. One was a *Sholayee,* a Mao Zedong communist; the second was an *Ikhwani,* a believer of the *Ikhwanu-l Muslimeen* Movement. The third teacher called himself a nationalist, not affiliated with any political party. The three teachers were in disagreement with Shear Zaman's ideology, which was in line with the Soviet Union Marxism-Leninism. Each one of the four would call the rest of the teachers as (national traitors) and agents of a foreign country, during their argumentative discussions in *gardab*.

Shear Zaman rounded up all three of his opponents in the first week of his appointment as the district governor. He planned to deal with them one by one.

"Ok, you national traitor," Shear Zaman addressed the *Ikhwani* teacher who was cuffed and brought down to the basement on a Friday night. "Where are your other *Ikhwanis*? I know you traitors are planning something to sabotage our people's revolution."

"I have not done anything against you," The accused replied in a bold voice.

"What is this? You son of a donkey," Shear kicked him on the head holding a night leaf to his face. "You called us the agents of the Soviet Union; you called us traitors Ha? You bastards." Shear threw another hard kick on the teacher's head as he became extremely frustrated when the accused, resisted confessing. He started throwing the rocks, which were there for this purpose, hitting him on the face and the head as hard as he could.

"You will not go out alive from here if you don't confess, you traitor. You better tell me where your other traitors are." Tufan took a deep breath as the teacher remained silent and stared at him angrily. He spat at the accused, left the basement and sent his young fellow, the "Legendary Revolutionary Boy," down to the basement to finish the job.

It was also the verdict of the Revolutionary Leadership that any dead body from the basement should be tossed in a deserted area, and not be given to their relatives. So the body was carried out in the middle of the night and tossed in the desert.

The *Sholayee* teacher– a follower of the Mao ideology, was next. Shear Zaman was particularly mad at this opponent because he was a charismatic activist. He always left Shear Zaman speechless during their debates about justifying their ideologies, and strongly defeated Shear Zaman to the point that sometimes the audience laughed at him.

"Now, tell me, you son of a donkey, who is the real revolutionary, you or me?" Shear questioned the prisoner triumphantly.

"The people will make the judgment soon," The *Sholayee* said boldly.

"The people did make their judgment already. Are you blind? Didn't you see yesterday and the day before that so many thousands of people poured into the streets by tens of thousands all over the country and welcomed the revolution?"

"You force the people, you intimidate the people to go out to the street and chant for you, but otherwise you will never prove that the masses of the people are with you."

"You are still the same stupid donkey as you were before, fuck your mother," Shear Zaman screamed, throwing a bigger rock on the teacher's face.

"You are the same traitors as you were before," The *Sholayee* said, spitting a mixture of blood and saliva on Shear Zaman, who was staring at him with extreme disbelief.

"In the name of the oppressed people of Afghanistan, you are convicted to be stoned to death," He chanted, throwing another big stone at his opponent's face. "There is no use arguing with you, son of a donkey."

The stoning to death of the diehard *Sholayee* was not an easy job; it took Shear Zaman a good one hour to finish. It made him extremely tired and therefore, scheduled the third enemy, the nationalist teacher for two days later.

"What do you think, you philosopher of nationalism? Don't you still believe in the Internationalism as the Soviet Union approved and supported the revolution of the people of Afghanistan?" Shear asked the cuffed teacher who had just been brought down to the basement.

"Tufan Sahib, I admit my mistake. Please forgive me. I really side with the revolution, and am ready to do whatever you ask me to." The teacher said humbly.

"Are you honestly saying this, or you are just scared?"

"Yes, I deeply believe in the revolution, especially when I saw that tens of thousands of our hard working and oppressed people that came out to the streets in support of the revolution. Now I firmly support our revolution; I am ready to sacrifice my life for safeguarding it."

"I will give you a chance to see how you behave. But what about your younger brother, he was also one of my opponents?"

"I know, he has a connection with some dangerous people. I haven't seen him for the last few days. I will inform you as soon as I find out his whereabouts." The teacher promised.

"Okay. Now I can trust you. In the name of the people of Afghanistan, you are pardoned. You will be soon allowed to go home. Make sure you inform me about your brother and stay in touch with me for some assignments, okay?"

"Yes, Tufan Sahib. I promise I will do anything you want me too."

Tufan took a deep breath out of satisfaction and lit a cigarette.

"Dear comrades," Tufan, the executive leader of the district, addressed the first session of the new revolutionary leadership committee of his territory.

"Today we are meeting here to celebrate the victory of the oppressed and hardworking people of Afghanistan. Now, we, the members of the People's Democratic Party of Afghanistan, are making the history of the country. Our most and foremost responsibility is to crush any resistance to the revolution and eliminate all those who are by nature opposed to it. We should be merciless to them. I would like to request comrade Noor, the intelligence chief, and comrade Nawab, the police chief to expand and enhance the security of the district by hiring stanch and loyal party members to the service so that no agent of the reactionary would be able to infiltrate in our ranks."

"Comrade *Wolaswal*," the inelegance chief said in a triumphant tone. "I can assure you and all my dear comrades that I will be working days and nights to ensure that anyone who commits sabotage against our revolution will be eliminated on the spot."

All other members of the committee spoke one by one and rendered their assurance to the committee that they will be ready to defend the revolution against any possible threat.

"I would like to give good news to the committee," Tufan said with a victorious smile. "That I already finished three of the enemies, Allahdad who was one of the biggest reactionaries, a drug dealer and a fierce opponent to the revolution. I also finished two other dogs, an *Ikhwani* and a *Sholayee* treaters."

The members of the committee congratulated each other on the news, and then Tufan read a short list of the names that were also considered number one enemies and should be tracked down as soon as possible. Tufan mentioned that among the enemies who had escaped, Murad, and the previous district governor and the police chief were the priority to be captured immediately. The meeting ended with a collective chanting of the slogans, "Long live the revolution of the people of Afghanistan, long live the People's Democratic Party of Afghanistan."

Within a year after he was appointed as the district governor, Shear Zaman Tufan established a good record of himself as a disciplined, effective and strong district governor and also as a ruthless partisan against the enemies of the revolution.

A month before the first anniversary of the "April Revolution," Shear Zaman made a quick trip to Kabul. Upon return, he held a working dinner meeting of the revolutionary leadership of the district at his residence. He was dressed in a red coat and black pants, white shirt, and red tie. His dark mustache and neatly shaved beard gave him the look of King Amanullah, who acquired the independence of the country from Great Brittan in 1919.

"Dear comrades," He said at the beginning of the meeting, holding his glass of Stolichnaya Vodka up for a toast. "Let's drink for the victory of our revolution, for the victory of our party and the health of the great leader of the oppressed people of Afghanistan!" He emptied his glass of Stolichnaya, lit up a cigarette and continued. "As we are going to celebrate the first anniversary of the glorious victory of our revolution, I have two good news to my comrades; the first news is that our revolution is progressing with steadfastness as it is guaranteed by the great Soviet Union, the cradle of the world proletariat revolution. Our International comrades are now the sole leaders of the world proletariat movement; I can assure you that in our lifetime we will be witnessing the disgraceful fall of the world imperialism, especially the fall of the American Imperialism."

"Victory to the great Soviet Union, death to American imperialism," the assembly chanted collectively as they were emptying their glasses of vodka.

"Dear comrades." Shear Zaman lifted up his second full glass. "The second good news that I have for you is that our wise and kind party leadership is sending your comrade, Tufan to Maimana as the provincial governor. I am so grateful to our dear leadership for giving me the opportunity to serve the people of Afghanistan and making me the provincial governor of Faryab right at the time that I am turning thirty years old."

"You deserve it, congratulations comrade Tufan, you are a real revolutionary, and happy birthday dear comrade!" A collective concerted applause came from the meeting.

Shear Zaman Tufan took his office as the new governor of Faryab in Maimana and convened the first meeting of the provincial party leadership in the evening of the following day at the gubernatorial residence. Following the meeting, he was received with a formal dinner and a generous party of drinking vodka, hosted by the then acting governor, a young revolutionary fellow. During the dinner party, the heads of all the government branches made remarks, and each one of them welcomed Tufan with complementary words such as "a brave revolutionary," "a real servant of the hard working people of Afghanistan", "a faithful party member," a "trustworthy comrade," and so on. Shear Zaman would listen attentively to these compliments, combing his mustache with the fingers of his lift hand and sipping his Vodka alternatively.

"Dear comrades," he said, puffing a long circle of smoke in the air. "I would like to thank you all my revolutionary comrades for your sincere and comradely sentiments towards me. I want to assure you all that like in the past, I will continue to sacrifice my life for the cause of the people of Afghanistan as long as I am alive. One of our first revolutionary duties is to eliminate the enemies of the people as we have to establish a new peoples' government where there will be no exploitation of the hard working people, and there will be no oppression. This noble goal will be achieved only after all the oppressors and exploiters are eliminated from the face of the earth." Shear concluded.

The next month of his regime as the provincial governor was marked by two extraordinary events.

First, he married a 28-year-old girl who had graduated from Maimana high school and was a staunch PDPA member. Before Tufan arrived in Maimana, she had been promoted to the post of Maimana city-committee leadership. She was the only female PDPA member who had made it to the high hierarchy of the party at the time. She and Tufan met during the first dinner party given in Tufan's honor. The two singles got a bit personal and intimate during the party, especially after having a couple of shots of vodka together.

Two weeks later, they threw a small wedding party at the governor's residence and became husband and wife. As for the size and the venue of their wedding party, both had agreed on the notion that revolutionaries don't care about the old traditions, and that they did not want to spend their valuable time for making huge preparation for the wedding as their time was dedicated to the " business of the people."

Second, on the tenth day of his and his wife's wedding, Tufan received the news that his brother Shear Alam, who had just been appointed as the District Governor of Almar, was killed by a roadside bomb while on his way home from work. His driver and two bodyguards, also PDPA members, were killed in the blast as well.

"I know this was the work of Murad, the big traitor," Tufan told his security chief.

Tufan ordered that his brother should be taken to his hometown in Ghazni and be buried there. He did not go to Ghazni to attend his brother's funeral but convened a one-day *fatiha* in his residence in Maimana.

Now, more than ever, Shear Zaman was very keen on having a strong intelligence service. He would personally review each and every intelligence report daily. He instructed all party members in the province to perform their "sacred duty" of gathering information on the reactionaries, especially on those "enemies of the people" who had lost their privileges under the revolution.

One day, Shear received a report that Murad had found and recognized the body of his brother, and mobilized his people to do everything possible to kill PDPA members and jeopardize the revolution. The report was followed by rocket attacks on some police posts as well as on the government supply lines around the city of Maimana. The attacks were increasing every day as the war against the Russians, and their backed government intensified all over the country. Shear became particularly enraged when one of the PDPA activists, a middle school teacher, was abducted, stoned to death and tossed in the same deserted area where Murad's brother had been tossed. Shear Zaman ordered a celebrated burial for the teacher and personally attended the procession.

"We will take revenge for the blood of our martyred comrade," screamed Shear Zaman at the funeral. "We swear we will come after you, the blood-thirsty enemies of the people of Afghanistan! We will kill as many traitors as possible to avenge for the sacred blood of our comrade, who sacrificed his life for the noble cause of the revolution!"

When a second teacher and party member was abducted and killed the same way, Shear Zaman went crazy and blamed his government and party inability to capture Murad.

"I am disappointed with the fact that our comrades are being abducted and killed by our ruthless enemies but we can do nothing. This is a shame; we must be able to get rid of this thug, Murad. I hereby order each and every one of the party members, each and every one of our intelligence and police forces, to be vigilant days and nights and go after this historic enemy of ours."

Tufan reported to the interior minister in Kabul that Murad was an "extremely dangerous enemy" and asked the minister to provide him more help to get rid of him.

On September 14, 1979, there was a change in the PDPA government leadership in Kabul. One of the "True sons of the people of Afghanistan"- Noor Mohammad Taraki was replaced (later assassinated) by his "Loyal Student" Hafizullah Amin. Amin was now called the True Commander of the April Revolution and "The brave son of the oppressed masses of the people." He was declared the General Secretary of the Central Committee of the PDPA and the Chairman of the Presidium of the Revolutionary Council of the Democratic Republic of Afghanistan. Shear Zaman was very quick to declare his loyalty to the new leader at the dawn of the change, and immediately convened an emergency meeting of the provincial party leadership.

"Dear comrades," He said. "Today our revolution has taken another step forward. We now have a more energetic and strong leader, the brave son of the people of Afghanistan: dear comrade Hafiz Ullah Amin. He is now the supreme leader of both our party and of our government. Long live Hafizullah Amin!"

Shear Zaman chanted, throwing up his right hand in the air, and carefully studying the faces of the other members of the meeting over the change. Shear also sent a congratulatory message to Kabul and promised his absolute loyalty to the new leader.

On the third day of the change, among other appointees, Shear Zaman's name was announced on the national radio and television as the Chief of North-West zone of the country with the full authority in administrative and military affairs. He made a hasty trip to Kabul to perform his oath of office before his boss Hafizullah Amin. Upon return to Maimana, he found himself the executive as well as the military chief for the provinces of Faryab, Jawzjan, Badghis, Balkh, and Samangan. He was thus able to take a wide range of decisions by himself, among them, to execute his opponents without the approval of the provincial party leadership.

Per the instruction he received from the new ruler of the country, one of the most immediate tasks was to filter the ranks of the PDPA for those elements who were very much attached to Noor Mohammad Taraki and might not be fully loyal to the new leader. Therefore, he began a series of trips to all the provinces under his authority and held meetings with the party leaderships, who were also the governmental leaders. He had one message to all.

"The good of the country and the good of our party dictate that we all must fully and unconditionally obey the orders of the Brave Commander of our Revolution, comrade Hafizullah Amin. We must put aside our personal beliefs and tendencies and become the true servers of the country under the banner of loyalty to the Supreme Leader of our Beloved Homeland. I am warning all those elements within the ranks of our party, who are hesitant or all canceling other ideas, that they will be thrown out of the ranks of the party, and eventually, be eliminated as there is no place for traitors in the ranks of our party."

After completing the full round of trips to all his provinces, Tufan had a long list of party members who were identified as the staunch followers of Taraki. These people were of the belief that Amin had murdered Taraki and hijacked the political power. Tufan started the purification process of such elements starting from his own staff in Faryab; the chief of police, the director of education, the heads of the agriculture and public works departments were the first to go. Some were let go from their jobs, some were detained and later executed. This was a long and continuous task as there were reports of disloyalty inside the party every day and made his mind so occupied that he rarely had the opportunity to attend to the affairs of the public. His trustee, Afzal, the "Legendary Revolutionary Boy" was now made responsible for all the administrative affairs.

In the meantime, the revolt against the revolution was getting intensified to the point that Murad, who had become the Mujahedeen leader in the northwest, was able to target the governor's residence with rocket attacks and to kidnap and kill several party members and teachers. Therefore, Shear Zaman lost patience with any minor resistance. He formed an execution squad in the North Wets Zone as he became paranoid and was quick to order the execution of the suspicious party members without doing even some preliminary investigation.

In the very last days of the year1979, there was a dramatic change in the political scene of Afghanistan. Under "Operation Storm 333," Soviet Union tanks roared into the country. Hafizullah Amin was killed, and Babrak Karmal, the leader of the Parcham faction of the PDPA, was brought to power by the Russians. The Parcham faction had been in hiding as Amin, who was the leader of the other faction of the PDPA called Khalq, considered Parchamis as traitors. Amin had tried to eliminate all Parchamis from the country's political scene. Its leadership was living in exile, hundreds of its members were arrested, and many of them were killed. Now it was the turn of the Khalqis to be removed from power, arrested and executed. Shear Zaman was one of those party activists who was seen as the staunch Aminists. He was called back to Kabul. He knew that he was going to be arrested and punished. Therefore, he escaped the situation and went into hiding. He went to his second cousin's house in a village in Ghazni province. His cousin was a peasant who was never involved in politics and not known to the PDPA circles. Shear Zaman stayed there with an as much low profile as possible. In the meantime, he gradually established ties with the new Parchami governor of Ghazni who was his classmate at the time when he was a middle school student. At that time, Shear Zaman himself was considered to be a Parchami as well. He tried to explain to his friend through messengers that he was simply a staunch supporter of the revolution and whatever he had to do during his era was simply for the good of the revolution. He explained that he had never been supporting Taraki or Amin personally.

To Shear Zaman's surprise, his protégé the "Legendary Revolutionary Boy" happened to be a secret Parchami follower and was installed in his place as the governor of Faryab. Shear Zaman had never suspected him to be a Parchami agent but was happy to see his student and trainee now in the position. He sent him a message, offering him his loyalty and help, but in return, he received an advice to stay in hiding and keep a low profile for a while more.

After the Red Army invasion, the situation in the country changed dramatically. The Mujahideen, who were fighting for the freedom of their country, were getting more and more ground among the people. The fighting spread almost to each corner of the country. The United States got involved; it provided generous support in the forms of arms and ammunition, financial and moral support as well as diplomatic support to the Afghan Mujahedeen. The Soviet Union who was suffering from severe economic problems, became under tremendous pressure by the International community to withdraw its troops from Afghanistan. Gorbachev, the Soviet leader, announced theatrical changes in the light of his policy of glasnost "openness" and perestroika "restructuring." It became obvious that the Soviet Union was seeking a face- saver to leave Afghanistan, and therefore devised a change of leadership and policy in Afghanistan. In late 1986, Babrak Karmal, under whom the division among the PDPA ranks widened and the situation in the country worsened, was deposed and replaced by another moderate Parchamite- Dr. Najibullah. Dr. Najibullah announced the policy of

National Reconciliation under which he tried to piece together the various factions of the PDPA and also opened the door for making peace with the Mujahideen.

Shear Zaman came out of hiding and made open contacts with the Najibullah followers. He first went to Faryab and met with his "Legendary Revolutionary Boy," who remained in his position as the governor of Faryab under Najibullah. He welcomed Shear Zaman and received him with respect. The situation in Faryab was as worse as it had ever been. The governor badly needed a strong man like Shear Zaman to help him. He proposed to the capital that Shear Zaman be used as an advisor to the governor in fighting the Mujahedeen. The proposal was approved and Shear Zaman was, thus running the governmental affairs in Faryab behind the scene.

But he was smarter than that to stay behind the scenes and envisioned a wider role for himself in the future of the country. He wanted to show to Dr. Najibullah that he was a staunch supporter of his policy of National Reconciliation. He started preaching the policy during meetings with the PDPA members as well as with the residents of Faryab. He planned many meetings with the people and scheduled interviews with media where he would passionately speak in favor of the National Reconciliation policy. His efforts finally earned him a higher place in the regime. He was selected as the member of the leadership of the High Council of the Homeland Peace Association.

As in the past, Shear Zaman's charisma helped him once again to earn a good reputation within the ruling regime, and this time promoted his image as a loyal national reconciliation champion. He would lecture party meetings about the benefits of, and the historic need for, national reconciliation. As the Geneva talks between Afghanistan and Pakistan under the mediation of the UN secretary general were in progress, and the national leadership was sending peace messages to the Mujahedeen leaders, he sent a secret invitation to Murad to come to the negotiation table and hold peace talks with him. In the meantime, however, he was pressing Afzal, the governor of Faryab, to go after Murad as harshly as possible so that he would be forced to come to the negotiation table. He was thus envisioning a credit for himself and hoping for a higher place in the future reconciliation government.

The reply he received from Murad was: "Get lost, you son of a Russian pig."

In a few months, with the help of his Russian advisor, Shear Zaman made several trips to Moscow, Berlin, and Prague. During these trips, he made several international friends.

In late 1988 Shear realized that the days of the Soviets in Afghanistan were numbered as the Geneva accord was signed by the two countries under which the Red Army was to leave the country. He was quick to think of a place for himself in Moscow.

In February of 1989, the last Soviet troops left Afghanistan and the Najibullah government was left alone in the fight with the Mujahedeen. The Najib's government stayed in power for almost four years, and Shear Zaman was active in the field of national reconciliation. But when the government fell to the Mujahedeen in 1992, Shear Zaman was among the first people who had already made his way to Moscow.

When still in Afghanistan, he was among the first people who made secret contacts with the North Alliance, a group of Mujahedeen who was fighting the Afghan government and the Soviet troops mostly in northern Afghanistan. His efforts to bring Murad to the negotiation table was also aimed at achieving this goal but it was futile; as the jihad was getting more and more momentum and by the passage of every day, Dr. Najibullah's government was sinking in disarray, Shear Zaman and his "Legendary Revolutionary Boy" made secret contacts with the commander of the North Alliance. In their message, the two mentioned that they were ready to join the alliance and help in establishing the Mujahedeen government after the fall of Najib's government. They pledged that they would bring along with them a large group of PDPA activists as well as non-party members to the side of the alliance and that they would hand over to it all the governmental resources of the province, arms arsenals included.

In return, they received this message: "You need to surrender unconditionally. You need to order your party members and governmental staff to cooperate with us. You need to stay in Faryab until our commander Murad takes over the full control of the province, and then in a due process, your fate will be decided upon."

"It seems to me that we will be put to trial or even killed without trial." Shear Zaman said to his comrade in confidence.

"I don't know. But one of my cousins is an aid to one of the Mujahedeen commanders in Kunduz province; I can contact him for help," Afzal suggested.

"I am not sure if anyone can rescue us. We should decide quickly or we might lose our lives."

Both were silent and thinking about their future as the Mujahedeen rockets were pounding the nearby areas.

"I think we should surrender and then go to some other area in the country and live as ordinary people," Afzal suggested again.

"No, comrade. That's dangerous because everyone knows us, they will come after us," Shear Zaman said.

"Dear comrade Tufan, I have always believed in your wise leadership and your perfectly right advice, and I still do."

"Thank you, comrade."

"So let's go to Kabul and get passports and go to Moscow, I think this is the only way that we can rescue our lives."

"Excellent idea," Shear Zaman pressed his friend's hand. "Do you know anyone in the passport office?"

"Yes, remember? I told you that one of my close friends is working in the passport department of the foreign ministry," Afzal said.

"Very good comrade," said Shear Zaman cheerfully. "Let's get ready as soon as possible."

Within a week Shear Zaman along with his wife and a little daughter, and his friend acquired service passports, and with the help of their Soviet advisor, they got a visa to the Soviet Union.

On a cold morning in February of 1992, Afzal, still officially in charge of the party and government affairs of Faryab province and Shear Zaman, still a high ranking official of the Homeland National Reconciliation Council loaded their luggage into a government Russian jeep and drove to Kabul airport.

In a few days, the Dr. Najib government fell to the Mujahideen, and the two quickly applied for political asylum in Moscow. The then government of Soviet Union granted temporary visas to Afghan refugees and asylum seekers but never allowed them to become citizens of that country. In a couple of weeks, the number of those Afghans who applied for temporary refugee visas in Moscow reached thousands; they were pouring from Kabul daily. They did not have the right to employment and they were not allowed to travel freely to different parts of the country. Under the umbrella of the United Nations High Commissioner for Refugees, they received minimal monetary assistance but generally lived a very poor life.

There were, however, some wealthy individuals and families who could afford to pay three thousand dollars per person to a smuggler to get to Europe, USA or Canada. Shear Zaman and Afzal were among those Afghans who had enough money to do so but they found out that there they could do a lucrative business and make money. So they arranged to start the business of smuggling Afghan refugees from Moscow to Europe or to Americas and Canada.

The Afghan refugees were mainly stationed in a poor neighborhood in Moscow called Sevastopol; the Sevastopol hotel was hosting refugees three times more than its capacity.

The authorities asked the refugees to have a representative who could act as a liaison between them and the refugees. Shear Zaman was chosen. And he selected Afzal as his assistance.

Shear Zaman, using his previous Russian friends and advisors, made connections with staff in the passport authority as well as in the Moscow International Airport. He spread the word among the refugees that three thousand dollars would take them to a prosperous life in the West. He established a network of smuggling refugees from their residence in Moscow to inside the Russian airplanes heading to western destinations. The network would include taxi drivers, travel agents, travel guides, police officers and staff in the airport. Shear Zaman and Afzal were taking care of getting the forging passports and visas part of the job themselves. In the first three-four years, they sent hundreds of individuals and families to the West, and they made hundreds of thousands of dollars.

CHAPTER 3

MULLAH JABAR

"We are the servants of the Allah Subhana Wa Taala, and we are the followers of the Prophet Mohammad, Peace be Upon Him!"

"We are the servants of the Allah, and we are the followers of the prophet Mohammad!"

Mullah Jabar was teaching his class of twenty Taliban-religious students age 13-18, at a Madrassa, located in the Qabli village of the Arghasan District in Kandahar province. He twisted a leather whip in his right hand and hit those students who did not repeat the lesson loudly enough.

"We are the servants of Allah Subhana Wa Taala, and we are the followers of the Prophet Mohammad, Peace be Upon Him!" The Taliban repeated the lesson while swinging back and forth. All dressed in white *shalwar kamis*, wearing white caps and black turbans.

"Taliban, this is your first lesson," Mullah Jabar explained, lingering around the group.

"We are ready to sacrifice our lives for Allah, we are the enemies of the *kafirs*!" the Taliban would repeat aloud their second lesson after their teacher.

Mullah Jabar struck one student on the back because the 13-year-old boy was not rocking back and forth while repeating the lesson. The tiny student, looking pale, would then rock faster, and in a full swing, repeated the lesson aloud. "We are ready to sacrifice our lives for Allah, we are the enemies of the *kafirs!*"

The students were sitting on a shabby carpet in a larger room in the building of Madrassa, a mud house, guarded by two armed Taliban. Mullah Jabar would sneak out of the room time to time to make sure there was no threat from the American and Afghan soldiers. He constantly instructs the two guards: "Boys, be alert! Let me know immediately whenever you see any trace of the infidels, ok?"

"Don't worry Mullah Sahib; we are vigilant." The two guards would assure him.

The sixty-year-old Mullah Jabar had been teaching the class for the last two years and was considered one of the best instructors among the Taliban, especially regarding discipline and harshness on those students who were a bit lazy or who were not capable of properly pronouncing the Arabic words of their lessons. Dressed in white *shalwar kamis* and black turban, he always reminded his students to wear white clothes and black turban so that, on the day of Qeyamat- resurrection, the angles will recognize them as the population of heaven. He also ardently emphasized to his students to grow as long beard as possible as it was the sign of being a male before the *Horris*.

"If you sacrifice your life for Allah, Allah will grant you a stay in heaven, ad then you will have at your disposal 70 *Horris*- the pretty and young female angles and *Ghilman*- the young, handsome male angels. You will be enjoying an abundance of all kinds of foods and fruits and juices, available to you every second you wish. Each one of you will be living like a king inshaAllah," Mullah lectured his students while combing his long gray beard with the fingers of his left hand.

"If you kill one *kafir*, you will become *Ghazi*, and Allah will grant you eternal stay in heaven, and you will be saved from the flames of the hell," Mullah announced loudly, pointing to the class to repeat. "If you kill one *kafir*, you will become *Ghazi*, and Allah will grant you eternal stay in heaven, and you will be saved from the flames of the hell," the class screamed cheerfully.

"If you kill one *kafir*, you will become *Ghazi*, and Allah will make available to you all kinds of delicious foods and fruits and juices in heaven," Mullah added loudly.

"If you kill one *kafir*, you will become *Ghazi*, and Allah will make available to you all kinds of delicious foods and fruits and juices in heaven." The class echoed their teacher.

Among his fellow Taliban, Mullah Jabar was nicknamed Mullah *Ghazab,* meaning rage, for being so absolute and tough on anyone not listening to him or not obeying him. In the madrassa class, he would not tolerate any carelessness and would punish harshly as possible anyone who behaved so.

"You son of *Kafir*," he shouted one day and struck with his leather lash a fourteen-year-old Talib who was not quick enough to do his ablution and join the rest of the class for the afternoon prayer. "I think your father and mother were like animals because they did not teach you to obey your Mullah," he hit the pupil on the legs with his heavy leather lash several more times.

Mullah Jabar called this class his most productive one as he identified five pupils from among the class to become suicide attackers. They five students were ages 14- 18, who demonstrated categorical dedication during the exercise of getting ready for the sacrifice. During the last month of the class, this group was housed in a single room in the madrassa. The mud building had two parts; the front part, used as a mosque, open for public prayer, and the back part, comprising a classroom, two bedrooms, and a bathing facility. The entrance to the back part of the building was located in the *Hujrah*, a private room in the mosque used only by the Mullah for his private time.

In the last week of the class, Mullah held private and one on one sessions with the group of five students in his private room. The session was held after the night prayer and would last until midnight. During these sessions, his job was to enhance further the special phase of the training aimed at unconditional preparation.

"Now you are my good children; you are the privileged servants of Allah. You are already assigned a place in *Jannate*-e- *Ferdaus*- Paradise. Allah is watching you every moment that you are preparing to make a sacrifice for Him. In the Holy Quran, Almighty God promised His honest servants like you a place in the heaven. Allah-o Akbar- God is great!"

The students repeated the chant. "Allah-o Akbar!"

During the session, Mullah Jabar also repeatedly recited those verses from the Quran that praised those who make sacrifices in achieving the satisfaction of Allah.

"This is the key to heaven after you make the sacrifice, you will be immediately taken to heaven by a pretty angel that will open the door for you and place you in your assigned place in heaven," Mullah said, demonstrating a large bronze key in his hand.

Each time when he was handing over one of the five students to the suicide attack planning staff, Mullah would say aloud, "I thank you Almighty God for making me able to prepare these five dedicated friends of yours to make a sacrifice for you and achieve your Almighty's satisfaction. I thank you for giving me the opportunity to present to you a gift of my honesty and dedication. I am sincerely wishing to give me the same opportunity that one day I sacrifice my life in the way these beautiful friends of yours are doing it today."

Despite all the satisfaction, Mullah Jabar felt with his performance as the trainer of suicidal Taliban; he was greatly suffering from an old complex of revenge. He dreamt of doing something very nasty to two of the people who let him down the most: Murad and Shear Zaman. Murad set him up with the Russian soldiers which changed his life forever. He lost his reputation as a respectable jihadi commander of the Hizb-e-Islami Party as the incidence put him to the trap of communists who tremendously humiliated him. He was forced to bow to the Russians and the Government that he submitted himself to them, was willing to shave his beard and his head and act as one of them in fighting Murad. But they never trusted him. He was beaten and disgraced severely. Now both of them were alive and have a good life in Kabul. "I will never have a dignified life and a bright future with the existence of the two who know my scandalous past," he repeatedly told himself.

From among the five good students that Mullah trained for suicidal attacks, two of them were a14 and a15-year-old boys from his own district. They were the grandsons of one of his longtime friends. The children's parents had been killed during a Russian bombardment over their village a year ago. And their grandfather dedicated them to the cause of Jihad. He told Mullah Jabar the day he was enrolling them in his class:

"These are the gift of Allah given to me; I give this gift back to Allah. I want them to do whatever can satisfy the Almighty God, and you are my brother I want you to train them and send them for the ultimate sacrifice."

Since that day, Mullah had had the two orphans in mind during the whole period of training for fulfilling his own wish of killing Murad and Shear Zaman. He would call them *Khoshbakhta Halokan* or lucky boys and always pay exclusive attention to them.

"I want you to send my "lucky boys" to heaven as soon as possible," Mullah told the head of the suicidal attacks planning group. "There is no better target than the two traitors and *kafirs*- Murad and Shear Zaman. I know their whereabouts and will help the boys in carrying out their mission,"

"Of course Mullah Sahib, I know they are our big enemies, we must get rid of them. I will send the boys to this mission as soon as I get the verdict from the judge," the head of the attack planning group assured Mullah Jabar.

After the two boys were given the instruction to kill Murad and Shear Zaman and Mullah Jabar was assigned to lead the operation, he picked Murad to go first and chose the senior brother to become a *Ghazi* and probably a martyred as well by carrying out the attack. Mullah Jabar volunteered to lead the operation himself and picked the Eid-ul-Fitr- a three-day religious holiday time for the attack as he knew that Murad would certainly be in Kabul for the holiday period. He was aware that both of his enemies had houses in Taimany-Kabul.

He and his boys traveled to Kabul by public transportation. They took place in a *samawar*- a teahouse in Taimany, from where they could see Murad's house and monitor his movements. The dining room of the teahouse was used in the night as a guesthouse, fitting a total of five people. Before ordering food and tea, Mullah told the teahouse owner that he was sick and would pay him extra money if he and his boys could reserve the place for the night. The owner, a single middle age man, agreed but with one condition:

"You look like a mullah, and maybe you will wake up early in the morning, I am tired because I worked the whole day, don't wake me up early in the morning for prayer."

"Do you want to sleep here with us?" Mullah asked, pointing to the area where they were sitting.

"No. I have a small room in the back.

"Ok, brother, I won't bother you, God is merciful. My grandsons and I are quiet people."

. Mullah decided to carry the attack on Murad in the morning of the first day of Eid, because he was confident that Murad would leave his house for *Eidgah*, the place of Eid prayer, in the morning and most probably he will walk to the place rather than driving as it was very hard to drive in the extremely crowded city, especially at the time *Eidgah*.

Mullah gathered his "Lucky Buys" close to him in the far corner of the teahouse, trying to keep them up for the night.

"Allah S.W.T is watching you that you are awake in the middle of the night that you are praying for Him and that you are preparing yourselves for making a sacrifice to achieve His satisfaction," Mullah Jabar was whispering to his "Lucky Boys" assuring them about the righteousness of their mission. He and the boys were performing the prayer of *nafal* when a police night patrol knocked the door, he saw the police through the cracks of the door and opened the door for them. The two policemen entered the teahouse hastily.

"What are you doing here? And where did you come from?" one police questioned Mullah Jabar

while still standing up.

"I am Haji Abdullah, and these are Mohammad Rasul and Mohammad Naqib, they are my grandsons. We came from Qalat to do the Eid prayer here in the morning and then go to the hospital for my leg, I have severe pain in my leg," Mullah Jabar wrinkled his face, demonstrated his artificial leg to the police, and then showed them his faked *tazkira*-National ID booklet. The boys followed their leader and showed their faked *tazkiras* to the police too.

"What are you and the boys doing in Qalat?" the police asked.

"I own a textile store there, and they are working with me after their school hours," Mullah Jabar lied again.

The police searched the room and everyone in it, including the teahouse owner who had also joined his guests with his eyes half open. The policemen left without finding anything suspicious. Mullah recited with himself a Doaa- prayer, thanking God for saving him and his Taliban from the police. It was around a few minutes later that Mullah heard the sound of a Land Cruiser across the wide street of the Taimany Road. He sneaked out through the teahouse entrance and saw a car stopping by Murad's house. Mullah silently praised himself for his prediction being right and whispered to the two kids: "Our target arrived as I predicted, you will become *Ghazi* tomorrow InshaAllah-God Willing;" Mullah pointed to the older boy.

It was around the early dawn when Mullah told his boys to get ready for the Morning Prayer, and a low voice knock was heard on the teahouse door; Mullah quietly opened the door and let his fellow Taliban member in. The man, not even uttering a word, handed over to Mullah a small size leather case, and before leaving Mullah and his "grandsons" alone, he raised his hands in the sign of praying for their success. Mullah and his kids hastily performed the Morning Prayer, after which Mullah immediately opened the leather case and equipped the boys with the explosives. The boys were already properly trained how to hide the explosives under their vests and the ignition wires under their sleeves. Mullah praised the boys for being quick and precise for managing everything but briefly tested them as to how to use them when the time comes.

Security was tight in the morning as the people walked to mosques for the Eid prayer. Armed police soldiers and armored vehicles were visible everywhere in the city.

"Be prepared son, the traitor is going to be out of his house any minute," Mullah instructed the senior of the two boys as the time was showing 8 AM and people started walking out of their houses going to the *Eidgah-* a huge mosque, around 20-minute walk from Murad's house.

Mullah Jabar and his boys were dressed in new clothes for the occasion of the Eid. They stepped out of the teahouse as soon as Murad appeared from his house walking toward the *Eidgah* along with his eight people entourage, some armed, escorting him on both sides.

The streets were crowded; people were walking in groups saying salaam and Eid Mubarak to each other on their way to Eidgah. Traditionally, people hug and kiss on the cheeks and juniors kiss seniors hands after the prayer of Eid, but juniors were not to be blamed for so doing before the prayer. Jabar and the boys crossed the street, walked behind Murad and his group. While keeping himself out of Murad's sight, Jabar quietly tapped and said goodbye to the assigned suicide attacker to separate himself from him and the other boy and get closer to Murad. The boy strode and mingled with another group of people who was walking right behind Murad's group. In the days of Eid, it is as if everyone knows everyone on the street. Everyone says salaam- peace be upon you, to everyone regardless of knowing or having seen them ever.

He was acting cheerfully, saying salaam to the people around him and kissing their hands.

"Eid Mubarak-HAPPY EID!" he would say aloud causing some people from Murad's group to look back at him and replied to him accordingly. As the group was getting closer to the *Eidgah*- the boy got faster, almost running toward the front of the group.

"Rayes Sahib Eid Mubarak!" He shouted with panic trying to approach Murad.

"Stop, you son of a bitch!" shouted Murad's younger son. In a blink of an eye, he held both of the boy's hands up and asked his brother who was walking next to his father to search the boy.

"Rayes Sahib, you go ahead with your prayer I will take care of this dog," Murad's younger son said to his father while defusing a bomb attached to the attacker's chest under his vest. He walked the boy to a police patrol car which happened to be stopped nearby and showed them his badge. He pushed the boy inside the vehicle violently and ordered the driver to take them to his own police station in the fourth precinct of the city of Kabul.

Murad's son was a seasoned police officer; he and his brother were off duty today, dressed in civilian clothes in order to accompany and protect their father on the way to the Eid prayer. In a few minutes of arrival to the fourth precinct police station, of which he was the chief, he tortured the boy brutally and made him confess everything.

"I was here to blow up myself and Haji Sahib Murad Khan. I was trained and brought to Kabul by Mulla Sahib Jabar,"

Mullah Jabar and the other boy quickly disappeared as they saw their boy was caught. A pickup truck waiting for them behind the stores along the road to *Eidgah,* picked them up and drove them to the Paghman District and then from there back to Kandahar. Jabar was too scared to stay in the capital and pursue the plans for killing Shear Zaman. During the stop in Paghman, he reported the situation to his authorities in Kandahar via a radio communication located in the outskirt of the district. He was instructed to disarm the other buy, leave the explosives there and go back to Kandahar through immediately.

Abdul Jabar, shortly known as Jabar, was born in a poor rural neighborhood in the Khakrez District of Kandahar Province. His father, Abdul Qahar, was known in the district as *Sagbaz* Qahar, or Qahar-the *dog player*. No one in the neighborhood had any idea what Qahar was doing for his daily life because he was never seen in public events such as weddings and funerals. He did not even attend the five-time prayer in the local mosque. But everyone was aware that he was one of the best fighting dog trainers in the whole area. In his village, there was a dogfighting show every Friday afternoon, and he was always there with his dog. Qahar was the one who would win the fight most of the times, and then collect the money that the spectators would bet on his dog.

Qahar was too busy with his dog fighting business, and never had time to manage to send his son, Jabar to the mosque for elementary religious studies as everyone else in the neighborhood did. Occasionally, he did try to take Jabar to the mosque, but Jabar would cut the class and leave in secret every time. He would not return to mosque until the Mullah reported to his father and his father would bring him again to the mosque. After a few trials, both his father and the Mullah were frustrated with Jabar and left him alone.

When he turned twelve, Jabar was out of his house most of the times, both days and nights. He spent his time playing the popular game of *Topedanda* for sometimes, but later he started playing the dangerous game of *Dornakhat* with his friends in the street. In this game, a group of boys was put in a circle drawn on the ground, and one person from outside the circle would strike the group by a hard rubber or even a soft metal lash, locally called *Khordom.* Each person of the group tried to kick that person and become a winner by hitting the lash-holding person by their foot and take over the lash and start striking the group by the whip including the previous winner (the person who was just outside the ring.). He was aggressive; he would fight with others over tiny things and beat them brutally. He formed a street gang called the Jabar Dallah- the Group of Jabar. As he grew up and became more aggressive, his group became known as the Jabar *pilochan-* Jabar's gang. Jabar would go around the streets, walking in front of his group, making fun of anyone who did not say salaam to him and sometimes kicking pedestrians and calling them nasty words.

Over time, Jabar's group gradually became so violent that all the neighbors and even the residents of the surrounding streets were afraid of them. At night, the group would go to the neighboring village of Zangabad and rob anyone who walked the streets in the dark. But when the residents stopped walking outside for fear of Jabar, the group started breaking into homes and steal things. One night he stole a bicycle from a home and took it to another neighboring village of Sperwan, where he sold it for 50 Afghanis. Now having some money in his pocket, Jabar went after a young boy of age 10, whom he liked, and offered 10 Afghanis for having sex with him. The boy refused the deal, but Jabar continued to bother him. The boy was related to one of the boys from a neighboring street that had once picked a fight with Jabar's group over their rudeness towards their elders. This time the boy came with a stronger group and with the plan to punish

Jabar severely. During their fight, Jabar's right arm was broken, and his group was beaten.

"Look, buddies," Jabar addressed his group one day after his broken arm got healed. "We are going to get these bastards and fuck their mothers okay?"

"Yeah, Jabar. Let's go now," echoed his group in concert. The group, comprising three boys, was armed with wooden sticks and *Khordom-*heavy metal whip. But Jabar took a sharp hunting knife with him.

"We fight until I tell you to stop, okay? And look, leave that tall bastard to me." Jabar instructed his group.

When the Jabar group met their rivals on their street, they were also three people, armed with similar weapons. The fight lasted a good twenty minutes. One of Jabar's friends was wounded badly, but Jabar was able to kill the tall boy that he thought had broken his arm.

Jabar was now a wanted man in the District of Karz and the province of Kandahar. But he had no place to hide. He and one of his gang who was also a home run away decided to flee to Quetta, Pakistan. It was easy for them to mingle with other Kandaharis there and make friends with them.

Quetta was a place of hideout for many Afghan murderers and other criminals who had fled the country. Jabar and his friend resided in a room with someone who came to Quetta a couple of years ago and now had a Samawr- teahouse in the Old Quetta Bazaar. This place was full of such Afghans, especially Kandaharies, like Jabar and his friend who escaped from jail or fled their homes for similar reasons.

Life was tough in Quetta for the jobless. Jabar and his friend started sneaking back and forth into Kandahar and made money by stealing, robbing and shoplifting. They would go back to Quetta enjoying the easy border crossing whenever they felt Kandahar was unsafe for them after stealing things. It was easy to sell stolen merchandise at a reduced price in Quetta. It was normal and a way of life for many.

One day an acquaintance of Jabar, who had met him at the teahouse, approached him. "How long do you want to go hungry around like this? Do you want a job?"

"Yes I do, give me any job, what is it?" Jabar asked enthusiastically.

"Are you sure you can do it?" The acquaintance asked.

"Is it *waradar*?" meaning lucrative.

"Yes, it is worth five thousand Pakistani Rupees for you and the same for me," the man said.

"Ok, tell me, what is it? I want to do it right now," Jabar insisted.

"What If you get caught, are you going to confess?"

"I am not a *sust!*"

"Ok, come." The acquaintance walked Jabar inside a market place in the Old Bazaar.

"Do you see that man?" asked the acquaintance pointing to a shopkeeper in the far corner of the marketplace.

"Yes."

"This guy has money. In the evening when he closes his shop, you and I come and finish him."

"Ok."

"I give you fifty Rupees now, go and eat a good *chainakee*."

Jabar grabbed the money hastily and went straight to the nearest teahouse and ordered a *chainakee* and hashish hookah.

In the evening, Jabar and his acquaintance went to the assigned place, hiding behind a mass of trash. They waited there until the target started counting his money and then closed his shop. It was dark, and except for one or two shops, the rest were closed. The target passed Jabar, not noticing him. Jabar attacked the man from behind with a long blade that his acquaintance had provided him with. The man fell to the ground, bleeding badly. Jabar and his friend quickly searched him, emptied his pockets and fled.

"Do you know Jabar who was that man?" asked the acquaintance once they got to their room.

"No."

"He was from Jabha."

"What is that?"

"It's a party of traitors. We are the true Mujahedeen; we need to kill them all."

"Ok, where is my money?"

"Don't talk about money anymore; there is none. Now you belong to the Hezb- e-Islami. You will be trained and sent to Afghanistan for Jihad to kill the Russians and their puppets. If you kill one of them, you will become a *Ghazi*, if you get killed, you will be a *Shaheed*, a martyr. In either case, you will be granted a stay in heaven, God willing."

"But I have nothing to eat," whispered Jabar.

"Don't worry; you will be given a lot of food, clothes and also weapons. Before going to Afghanistan, you will be going to a training camp In Peshawar soon."

Jabar was concerned as to he would be able to show up in Afghanistan and not get caught for murder, but also excited at the thought of getting heavy weapons in his hands.

But now he had no choice. He had heard the stories of those Afghans who were killed for refusing to join the Hezb-e- Islami for Jihad.

It was the winter of 1979 when the Red Army poured into Afghanistan under the pretext of combating American Imperialism. The then ruler Hafizullah Amin was murdered, a new leader by the name of Babrak Karmal was installed. The new leadership announced some measures to form a national coalition and to bring the warriors into the peace process. But the war had gotten further momentum. The insurgency spread to all corners of the country. The Hizb-e-Islami was active in and around the city of Kandahar. For this reason, Jabar was assigned to Kandahar, specifically to his home district of Khakrez.

Once in the Khakrez area, Mujahid Jabar, now armed with heavy machine guns and supported by the strongest Jihadi party of Hezb-e-Islami, started looking for the remaining two rivals with whom he had the street fight before he left for Pakistan. Jabar found out that one of them was working as a *pyadah,* an office servant, doing mail and janitorial duties in the office of the Director of Education of the district. The other was doing a similar job in an elementary school.

"I am going to get rid of the education director who is a *Parchami,*" Jabar told his post commander.

"Yes, yes. Go finish that son of an infidel," said the commander.

Now that Jabar had the okay from his boss to finish the education director, he asked the commander to give him two other Mujahedeen to help him in this mission. He got two men and planned to do the job the next morning when the director was going to his office. Jabar and his men arrived at the education director's office early in the morning and hide behind the adjacent building. The servant arrived earlier thirty minutes before any other employee arrived, and started cleaning up the director's office room, located in a single story small building.

"How are you, you son of a bitch?" Jabar said to the servant while entering the room and showing his Kalashnikov hanging over his right shoulder, covered by his *dopata*.

"Salaam Alaykum Jabar, how are you?"

"Cheshsh, be quiet. Come down with me." Jabar dragged the man out of the room and took him to where his other two men were waiting.

"This bastard is the servant of the *Kafir*, hold him here," Jabar instructed the two.

They kicked him on the buttocks a couple of times and threatened to be quite.

When the director's car arrived, a few other employees were also entering the office. Jabar whispered something in servant's ear.

"Salam Sahib, come here somebody wants to see you." the servant said to his boss, trying to act normally.

"Salaam, who wants to see me?" the director asked while walking toward his servant.

Before the man answered, Jabar and his men appeared, showed their weapons to the director and instructed him to get in the back seat of the car.

After finishing this job, Jabar was trusted with more important tasks. He was hot-blooded, energetic and ruthless. Now being a Mujahid, he tended to change his appearance. He grew his beard longer; his hair was as long as a woman's, which gave him a look of a philosopher. He tried to learn and memorize some verses of the Quran, so he could recite them whenever there was an encounter with Mullahs. He would also need to learn the Salaat, the five-time daily prayer, which he did not learn before.

In the mid-1980s, after the war against the Russians troops in Afghanistan escalated, Jabar got busier with Jihad, and in the meantime, he felt the need to become a Mullah so that he could do the imamate, gaining the authority as a religious leader and the ability of performing the Salaat prayer with his group of Mujahedeen. He instructed the Mullah of the local mosque in the area under his control to go to his post daily and teach him preliminary religious lessons. He would sit down with the Mullah and learn the basics of Islam for an hour every day. After a couple of weeks of study, he instructed his mentor to entitle him as mullah so that he could perform the imamate, and officially declare him a qualified mullah. The ceremonies for the announcement were held at the post with the participation of hem, the Mullah, and ten of his fighters. The Mullah put a new black turban over Jabar's head and officially declared him Mullah Jabar. From now on Jabar got the religious authority for issuing Fatwa- Islamic decree. With this new power, Mullah Jabar was in the position of issuing his judgment over the execution of any enemy captured by Mujahedeen during their fight.

Later on, he took an active part in quite a few successful operations, and he was seen by the high authorities of his party leadership in Quetta as a disciplined, tough, courageous and a die-hard warrior. In early 1986, on the recommendation of his boss, Mullah Jabar got promoted to the position of the post commander. Now it was Mullah Jabar who would decide the map of the operation in his area.

On his first day in his new post, he told his followers, "You know, school is the biggest source of infidelity in the country. It is a school where the communists teach and produce *kafirs*. I don't like those bare-headed bastards walking to school in the morning and going back home with their heads full of anti-Islamic shit in the afternoon. So we should kill all who are teaching or working or studying at school."

"Allahu Akbar. God is Great," chanted the rest of his men. "We should cut their heads off."

For a month or so, Jabar devised plans for kidnapping teachers, but there were PDPA members among the teachers who were armed with pistols. Mullah Jabar was not satisfied with the kidnapping of only a couple of teachers who were nonparty members but were teaching at the school just to make their living. He, however, got useful information from the captives about the home addresses of some of the teachers and about the situation inside the school. They told him that the PDPA members were armed and they were patrolling the school's surrounding during the nights. They estimated the number of the night guards about six teachers and four ninth- grade students.

From the very beginning of talking about getting rid of the school teachers and students, Mullah Jabar had his street rival in mind as well. He remembered when fighting with the group of three, this guy was the one that he was afraid of the most because he was heavy and had kicked him badly in the stomach. According to the captive teachers, he was now a PDPA member; he was armed and was staying in the school overnight. He and other night guards were assigned an office room in the school for sleeping in it.

By day, Mullah Jabar's frustration elevated. He tried to convince his superiors that all the communists in the school were staying in the school overnight, that they are doing prostitution with small school children and that this school was the training center for communists around the District of Khakrez. This way he got the authorization to make a decision about the fate of the school. Mullah Jabar planned a night raid on the school with firing one hundred rackets on it on a Friday eve "when the prostitution was on" as Mullah Jabar would put it.

After Mullah Jabr carried out the attack, it was announced over the government radio and television that there were two teachers and a *chaprasi* killed who were guarding the school, and the building of the school was reduced to rubble.

The party, to which Commander Mullah Jabar belonged, was known to be one of the strongest Mujahedeen parties and was receiving the lion's share of the western military and financial aid. This party was especially favored by American politicians such as Senator Charles

Wilson, who was very active in supporting the Afghan Mujahideen and the catalyst of providing the US aid to them. The other strong and the internationally favored party was the North Alliance, a coalition of Jameyat-e-Islami party and some armed groups from the north part of the country. Murad belonged to this organization. This party was particularly favored by France and was also receiving a big chunk of the US aid. The rivalry between the two parties was at every level, which would sometimes lead to armed clashes between them. In the mid-1980s, during a fierce fight between the two parties, the commanders from Mullah Jabar's party killed 16 commanders from commander Murad's party in Northern Afghanistan. Mullah Jabar was one of the commanders who took part in this fight and had been stationed in Faryab province- in the district of Andkhoy, where Haji Murad was the leading commander of the Northern Alliance party.

"You need to surrender to my forces or you will face severe consequences," Commander Mullah Jabar ordered Commander Murad through a private messenger.

Commander Haji Murad replied to his message by returning the dead body of his messenger, tied on the back of a donkey.

Mullah Jabar was enraged by the act of Murad and planned a secret attack. But the other party had already made its own revenge plans. Mullah Jabar was caught by surprise as Murad's people ambushed his commanding post on a cold rainy night following the killing of the messenger. During this encounter, most of Mullah Jabar's Mujahideen were killed, some captured, and Mullah Jabar himself was injured on the right leg during a rocket attack.

Humiliated by the defeat, Commander Jabar asked for backup. He refused to be taken to Quetta for the treatment of his injury. "I can fight with one hand, one leg and one eye," he said to his boss in Quetta, over a radio. "Don't worry about me, just send me some more men and weaponry I will finish this national traitor Murad in one day."

As a tactic, commander Jabar ordered his people to retreat to the hills in the eastern part of Andkhoy but making speedy preparations for the next battle in the meantime. He was impatiently awaiting the arrival of help and would insist on getting it when talking on the radio with his boss in the military chain of command in Quetta twice a day.

"Be patient, Mullah, you will receive different news soon," Jabar was told over the radio after two weeks of the retreat.

"Fuck your shit news, I don't need any news. I need men and guns," Mullah replied.

"We have reached a truce and a peace agreement with the Northern Alliance," an announcement over the radio said. "I hereby order all Mujahedeen of the Hezbe-e- Islami to observe the truce, stay in their posts and refrain from attacking the forces of the Northern Alliance except in self-defense. Both parties agreed to join forces against the Russians and their puppets."

Upon the receipt of this instruction, commander Jabar was mad at the beginning but gradually settled down with the peace agreement.

One day, sitting on a flat rock in his post, enjoying the warming rays of morning sunshine, he saw a motorcycle driving toward him. He rose and ordered his group to be prepared for a possible battle, but the two men on the motorcycle waved a white cloth as they got nearer. When the motorcycle arrived, the back passenger walked toward commander Jabar carrying an envelope in his hands.

"Salaam Alaykum, brother commander, here is a message from brother commander Murad to brother commander Jabar," the man said, handing the envelope over to Jabar.

Jabar handed the envelope to one of his people who was good at reading and listened to him reading the letter.

"Salaam Alaykum, brother commander Jabar," the man read. "As you know our leaders made peace with each other, which I fully agree with, and am complying with. Now you and I, as Muslim brothers, should come together in fighting against the infidels. Therefore, I am inviting you and five of your brother Mujahedeen to a brotherly and friendly party at my castle this coming Thursday night. I will send you a guide to direct you to my castle on Thursday evening. Be careful about the Russian patrol, leave in the dark. I hope you accept my initiation, commander Haji Murad."

"This son of a dog is scared of us already," Jabar commented on the invitation. But he quickly made a radio call to Quetta about this invitation. In a couple of hours, he received their okay to accept.

"Salaam Alaykum, brother commander Murad," Jabar said in his letter sent to Murad by messenger. "We will come to the party, but make sure you don't break the truce agreement."

Jabar and his five people armed with Kalashnikovs got into their old Toyota pickup truck and followed a motorcycle guide sent by Murad toward South Andkhoy.

Murad personally welcomed Jabar at the gate of his castle, and hugged him and took him to the inside hand to hand. Murad was accompanied by five of his armed fighters.

Dinner was served quickly. A servant from brought in a portable sink and water pot, and poured water on everyone's hands. The food was plentiful and delicious; it satisfied the hunger of Jabar and his people who had not had sufficient food for the last two weeks. Large bowls full of fresh pieces of homemade bread topped with lamb soup and meat, platters full of roasted chicken and *qabili pallaw,* rice topped with sautéed raisins and slices of carrots, was a standard dinner given to dignitaries, and Mullah Jabar realized that he was treated as such by his counterpart. Mullah Jabar ate so much food that he could not hold himself straight over the mattress, so he had to lay down and leaned his left elbow on a pillow.

"What do you think, Mullah Sahib; we all have been very tired and deprived of a good time for a long period of time, do you like to have a little fun?" Commander Murad asked, taking off his *pakol* from his head and putting it down by his side.

"What kind of fun, Haji Sahib?" Commander Jabar asked with amazement.

"Well, just traditional fun the people do here. I think you guys do it too in Kandahar, right?" Murad could tell Jabar still didn't understand. "Here when we people are tired and bored, we have some young boys who come and play around with a little music," Murad said.

"Ha! Yes, now I understand, yes Haji Sahib, if you like, I like it too," Mullah Jabar whispered with a slight smile on his lips covered by his mustache and beard.

Murad pointed to one of his people to go ahead and bring the music band in.

One man carrying a local drum and another carrying a *Tamboura,* a local stringed instrument, entered the large room, followed by two handsome boys, ages 12 or 13. The young boys were tall, had long hair, and dressed like girls in red skirts and colorful blouses. Each one of them was carrying over their feet above the ankles a pair of colorful *pizeabs,* a decorated set of light chains capable of producing rhythmic musical sounds when dancing. Mullah Jabar sat up and straightened himself in his place as the boys entered the room. He watched the handsome boys spinning around and shaking their backs, dancing girlishly.

"Do you have a smoke?" Mullah Jabar asked one of Murda's people referring to hookah.

"We have every kind of smoke, what do you like, Mullah Sahib? Tobacco or hashish?" the man asked.

"Bring in anything Mullah Sahib wants," Murad ordered his man.

Mullah Jabar inhaled a long smoke of hashish as the dancing party got hot and the boys danced seductively in front of him. At one point, Mullah Jabar could not control his excitement and grabbed one of the boy's hands, pulling him close. The boy pulled himself back with a girlish smile. But when he approached Jabar the next time, Jabar extended his hand toward boy's bottom. The boy pulled back again, turning his back to Jabar and shaking his bottom.

Mullah Jabar swallowed. Commander Murad smiled.

The dancing party went very well. Jabar was extremely happy and excited.

It was around three in the morning when the party was over. Murad advised Jabar to stay in the castle and get some sleep until the early morning so the Russian patrol would not make trouble for them. But Jabar preferred to leave in the dark of the night so that he could get to his post and then pack up and go back to the nearby village where he was instructed by his boss to stay until further notice.

"Thank you for coming, Mullah Sahib. May God be with you," Murad saw him off at the gate of his castle.

"Thank you Haji Sahib; we had very good time with you. May God be with you too," replied Jabar, getting into the passenger seat of his truck.

A day after, they moved to their previous post station in the nearby village in the middle of the night. Apparently, the villagers received Jabar and his people well, especially because they were no longer making trouble for them by firing at the Russian caravans who would time to time patrol the area. But on the second night of their stay, Jabar was caught by surprise when the village was raided by the Russian and governmental troops. Most of Jabar's fighters were killed, and he and his driver were caught while trying to flee the area in their truck, and taken to the district governor's office handcuffed.

"Murad betrayed you, you coward!" said Shear Zaman Tufan, the district governor of Andkhoy, accompanied by a Russian officer.

Mullah Jabar looked up at Shear Zaman brazenly but said nothing. "You son of a bastard," he thought of Murad.

"Talk to me, you bastard," Shear Zaman shouted at him, and punched him in the head.

"Give me one chance, I am going to cut his head off," Mullah Jabar said humbly.

"Give him one chance, ha! He wants a chance," Shear Zaman sneered, turning to the Russian officer with the translation of what Jabar said.

The Russian officer received the offer seriously and whispered to Shear Zaman to leave Jabar alone for the time being and talk about him later.

Jabar was taken to a special room in the headquarters of the Russian troops and was treated fairly well. Shear Zaman and his Russian boss discussed Jabar's offer and concluded that they can use him in an attack against Murad's forces.

During the interrogation, Mullah Jabar gave them important information not only about Murad's forces but also about his own party forces and their future plans in the area. Mullah Jabar received medical treatment by a Russian doctor in a local paramedical facility. He was kept in seclusion for two weeks. He was provided good food. Besides, a Russian officer in charge of the propaganda affairs would lecture him for an hour every day about the benefit of helping the government. After three weeks, it was decided that he should be sent to the frontline of war to fight Murad.

"I will kill Murad himself; you send me to the war front" claimed Mullah Jabar.

"You know that we will kill you and your body will be cut into pieces if you betray us," threatened Shear Zaman.

"I swear to Allah that I will not do such a thing," Mullah Jabar muttered.

"What is your idea about going after Murad, I mean how can you get him?" A Russian officer asked the question, translated by his interpreter.

"I will dress like one of the ordinary villagers, using a fake name, and contact his people that I want to become their fellow Mujahid," Jabar said.

"What if they already know you by face?" asked the Russian officer.

"I don't think any of the men in this province or any of Murad's people ever saw my face," Mullah lied, trying to assure the Russian who was staring at him with distrust.

"Shave your beard, and then they will not even suspect you," suggested the Russian officer.

Mullah Jabar was quiet for a moment, put his head down then up and nodded in agreement, but said suddenly, "All the villagers have beards, how can I shave my beard?" inquired Jabar.

"We will shave your head too and then tell them that you were a government soldier and fled your post to join them, we will give you the uniform," the Russian said.

Before the Mullah could say anything else, a Russian soldier entered the room and whispered something in his officer's ears. The officer left the room.

The Russians received instruction from Kabul to send Mullah Jabar to the Policharkhi prison in Kabul, as he was categorized the#1 dangerous enemy of the revolution. The capital also wanted to use Mullah Jabar as a bargaining point with the Mujahedeen in the effort to bring them to the negotiation table. He was transported by a Russian military helicopter to the Bagram airport and then carried to the prison by a Russian armored vehicle. In the prison, he was locked in a heavily guarded cell for a month, where he was never visited by anyone from the prison authorities. He was confused by the fact that back in Andkhoy he demonstrated to the Russians that he was ready to join the government forces and fight Murad, but now they treat him in such a harsh way. "Maybe they see me as a very important person," he said to himself.

"Come with me, Mullah Sahib," said a police lieutenant who opened the door to his cell in the middle of a cold winter night. Mullah Jabar stared at the officer in surprise. The officer extended his hand and grabbed Mullah's hand, pulling him out of the cell. The officer directed him to a Russian Jeep that was stopped close by with its ignition running; both, Mullah Jabar and the officer got into the jeep and left the prison.

In the morning, Mullah Jabar found himself in a clean, well-furnished office, greeted by a man in his early fifties, who was dressed in a black suit and white shirt.

"Welcome, Mullah Sahib," said the man. "I am the vice president of the High Council of the National Homeland United Front of Afghanistan. I was told that you have made the wise decision to join the people of Afghanistan and stop fighting the government."

"Yes, I told them in Andkhoy that I wanted to join the government, I didn't understand why they put me in the prison here."

"I don't know either, why they put you in prison, I think somebody made a mistake about you. But now you are a free man. We appreciate your decision, which I am sure will achieve the satisfaction of God and the oppressed people of Afghanistan. We will help you to live a peaceful life; you will be staying in a decent home and will receive financial assistance from the government."

"What is your job?" Mullah Jabar asked.

"Well, the job of the National Homeland United Front is to bring all factions of the Afghan society together and promote the peace process. You know, our country is ruined by the years' long war, there are some strangers who are interfering in our affairs, and therefore the government of Afghanistan decided two years ago to form this organization for the purpose of promoting peace among all Afghans and bring unity among them."

"Are they going to give me a house?" Mullah Jabar tried to hide his enthusiasm.

"Yes. Very soon they will give you a decent place," the man said and introduced to him a young man who had just entered the office. "This is my assistant; he will accompany you outside to the front of the building where you will be met by some journalists."

"What am I going to say?" Mullah asked.

"Don't worry; there will be ten more Mujahedeen out there who also decided to abandon the enmity with the people of Afghanistan. Every one of you will be given an empty machine gun, and you will put them down on the ground in the gesture that you are joining the peace process and no longer want to kill your innocent people."

"Kindly come with me Mullah Sahib." The young guy pointed to Mullah Jabar, opening the door for him and guiding him to the front of the building, right by the gate where a board says the name of the building as the National Homeland United Front. Mullah Jabar was placed in the front row, in the middle of a group of the people pretending as Mujahedeen with long beards and their bodies wrapped in their traditional cloth *dopatas*.

A newscaster with a microphone in his hand appeared.

"Dear viewers, what we see here is a large group of the Mujahedeen under the leadership of one of the well-known commanders from the Hezb-e-Islami party who put down their weapons and joined the government of the people of Afghanistan and the peace process. Here is their Commander Mullah Jabar."

The newscaster brought the microphone closer to Jabar's mouth.

Mullah Jabar was in a panic: his face was going to be shown on the national TV, and his voice broadcast on the radio and had no choice but to go ahead and talk to the microphone.

"By the name of Allah, the companionate, the merciful, I was a commander for the Hezb-E Islami party; I wanted to stop fighting the government and to come to the side of the people and join the peace process."

"What is your message to other people who are fighting the government?" questioned the newscaster.

"I want that they too stop fighting and ruining their country, and come and join the government in building our country."

After the interview, Mullah Jabar belonged to the National Homeland United Front of Afghanistan and was housed in a government controlled guesthouse with tight security. In his room, he had a TV set and watched himself talking to the microphone, in the primetime newscast that night. He realized that he should be already condemned to death by the leadership of his party as he was aware of the way it was treating defectors. He envisioned himself being hanged on a power pillar in the Old Quetta bazaar and people watching his dead body.

Jabar was having a good life in Kabul; he was living in a decent dwelling, receiving good food, and adequate monthly allowance. He would be transported in a new model Volga from his residence to the venues of meetings, organized by the NHUFOA. He would rarely agree to deliver a speech at such meetings though. "Where are you Jabar? What is this all about?" he would sometimes ask himself teasingly. He enjoyed life, and liked his position but never stopped wishing to escape it because he knew the Hezb-e-Islami was after him.

His fear intensified when the Russian troops decided to withdraw from Afghanistan in early 1989, and the government he was supporting was left alone in the face of internationally supported and ever growing power of Mujahedeen. He gradually distanced himself from the assigned activities as the member of the NHUFOA. One time he traveled to India for medical treatment and spent two weeks in New Delhi. Upon return to Kabul, he requested a one on one meeting with the chairman of the NHUFOA.

"I am feeling like I am under house arrest in Kabul. I have never been allowed to travel freely in the country." Commander Jabar complained.

"Is that the case?" asked the chairman of the NHUFOA.

"Yes sir, I have never been allowed even to go out of my residence without the company of an intelligence agent."

"I was not aware of that. In my eyes, you have been a respected member of our organization. Thank you for sharing with me this issue, I am going to talk to the authorities soon, and hope everything will be fine."

"Yes, I want to go out to talk to other people and bring them to the government side."

"I know, I know, Mullah Sahib, you are a patriotic clergyman, I have a lot of respect for you, and will certainly do something about solving this problem."

"God bless you, sir."

But the country's intelligence service had already been suspecting that Mullah Jabar was sharing information about the situation in the country with a foreign intelligence, namely ISI, the Inter-Services Intelligence of Pakistan. This suspicion was reinforced when he was visited several times in New Delhi by an Afghan merchant who was seen by the KHAD- the State Intelligence Service of Afghanistan as an ISI informant. Therefore, the same day the chairman of the NHUFOA asked for a meeting with the KHAD chief to discuss with him Mullah Jabar's request, he had already been taken out of his residence with his hands cuffed.

Jabar was repeatedly beaten and waterboarded by KHAD almost every day. He was not allowed to sleep the first two nights and was kept hungry. But Jabar would never confess his connection to ISI because he knew that confession equaled to death. After two weeks of torture, he was released at the constant request of the NHUFOA leadership. The leadership insisted that Mullah was an honest man and a good asset for the peace process in Afghanistan. Therefore, the Leadership asked that he be released and apologized to. The NHUFOA leadership succeeded in releasing Mullah Jabar from jail as the drum of National Reconciliation policy was being beaten loudly by the regime, and the government tried to demonstrate its commitment to the process.

Jabar was released under the condition that he never tells the story of his arrest and torture by KHAD to anyone. He was taken back to his previous residence. Two weeks later he was even sent to Tajikistan for treatment and getting rest there for the period of three weeks.

One year later, in 1992, the government of Dr. Najib fell to Mujahedeen, Dr. Najib went to hiding in the United Nations headquarters in Kabul, and the chief of KHAD committed suicide. Mujahideen took over; they freed all war prisoners, Mullah Jabar included. He went straight back to Quetta, where he tried to revive his old connections with the Hezb-e-Islami. But the party did not trust him easily, and they tried to avoid him. He told everyone in Quetta that the reason he once had stayed on the side of Afghan government was to get inside information and relay it to his party. After he received a cold reaction from his party, he started doing business; purchased a teahouse in Quetta with the money he had saved during his stay in Kabul.

But ISI never let him alone and continued to keep him in their spectrum of relationship. During the almost four years of Mujahedeen government in Afghanistan, the organization watched Mullah Jabar and encouraged him to go to religious studies. So besides supervising his business of teahouse, he would attend the madrassa in Quetta four hours a day. His teahouse became a gathering place for his fellow religious students at the madrassa.

The government of Mujahedeen proved to be an insufficient one. There was a fierce power struggle among the Mujahedeen parties inside Afghanistan, the inner fighting among the largest Mujahedeen parties, particularly between the Hizb-e-Islami party and the North Alliance made the whole country in complete disarray. The ISI saw this situation as in opportunity for itself to help bring about a government in Afghanistan that would be under their control.

Therefore, it mobilized Afghan religious students under the name of Taliban. ISI provided military and political training to the Taliban in order to prepare them for a government takeover of the country. Mullah Jabar, though not an advanced religious student, became one of the leading figures in the Taliban movement.

In 1996, the first group of Taliban was dispatched to Afghanistan under the umbrella of a caravan carrying trade merchandise from Quetta to Turkmenistan via Kandahar. Once inside Afghanistan, the caravan got involved in politics, made contacts with local tribal and religious leaders, and declared the campaign for the takeover under the name of restoring safety and security as well as establishing the Islamic Emirate of Afghanistan. The Taliban quickly took over Kandahar and other areas of the southern and western parts of the country.

Before the Taliban took over the whole country, Mullah Jabar was appointed the commander of Helmand Province. He was stationed in the capital city of Lashkargah. The province of Helmand was known as the center of opium production in the country, and Mullah Jabar quickly started collecting revenues from the opium growers. He, later on, established a command post for all drug operations. A refinery was put in place, which produced the finest material from the poppy and then transported to foreign countries. One of the routes to transport the opium was the route to Herat, where Murad had been operating for a long time. Mullah Jabar contacted Haji Murad to form a partnership in smuggling the materials to South Asian countries. Haji Murad, no longer an active Mujahedeen fighter, was controlling the drug trafficking route from Faryab to Turkmenistan. He declined the partnership at the beginning, but once the Taliban conquered the important city of Mazar-e-Sharif, followed by taking over most of Northern Afghanistan, Haji Murad had no choice but to accept the partnership.

Mullah Jabar and Haji Murad expanded the operation by building more advanced refineries. They were enjoying freedom in the business.

The drug business was the main source of the Taliban finance. It was so important that the leadership of Taliban would summon Mullah Jabar time to time to their headquarters in Kandahar and receive from him the complete report of the operation. They would urge the commander to make sure the revenue from the business increased as the expenses of the regime were tremendously exceeding their income. Therefore, Mullah Jabar would personally travel along the transportation route and meet with Haji Murad and other local drug dealers. This time Haji Murad was one of those people who met with the chief of the drug operation of the Taliban regime.

"Come on in Haji Sahib," Mullah Jabar said, welcoming Haji Murad at his residence located in the provincial compound of the Faryab governor. "We are no longer enemies; we are now the servants of the Islamic Emirate of Afghanistan, right?"

"Yes, Mullah Sahib," Haji Murad said, opening his arms to hug Mullah Jabar.

"I can pardon you for what you have done to me in the past. Allah likes forgiveness," Mullah Jabar said still holding his guest's hand in his.

"I swear to God that I had done nothing bad to you. You might have been thinking that it was me or one of my people who reported to the Russians after you left my house that night."

"That's fine Haji Sahib; God bless good Muslims, let's now do good to our Islamic Emirate."

During their friendly meeting, the two Mujahids, the two masters of the drug operation, discussed the safety of the operation and ways of expanding it. At the end of their meeting, Haji Murad presented a bundle of United States dollars in the amount of $50,000 to Mullah Jabar as his contribution to the cause of the Taliban. Mullah Jabar accepted the gift with appreciation. Haji Murad knew that in order for him to stay alive and to keep his business running, he needed to appease his partner.

As a Taliban commander, Mullah Jabar was considered an aggressive and decisive man. He would never hesitate to follow orders from his superiors. The first thing he did when he arrived in Faryab was to close down the schools. He then made immediate preparations for burning the middle school, which had been ruined once before, and burned it down to ashes once gain.

"Now I am going to bring true Islam to Afghanistan," declared Mullah Jabar at the receipt of a decree by the Chief of Taliban movement appointing him as the head of the southern zone of the newly formed ministry. "From now on all the girls' schools should be closed, every man has to grow a fist size beard, and the women should be barred from walking outside their houses without the company of a male relative."

The Taliban regime formed a Ministry of the Promotion of Virtue and the Prevention of Vice, under which Mullah Jabar was operating with an absolute authority in the provinces of Kandahar, Helmand, Farah, and Zabul. His boss had told him that he was entrusted this position because he was considered one of the true Muslims.

He put religious police on the street of the provinces to watch every citizen to ensure the obedience of the edicts and decrees issued by *Amir-ul Momeneen*, the supreme leader of Taliban. They would force people to close their shops and go to mosques five times a day for daily prayers. Anyone who defied the instructions would be beaten in public. Listening to or playing music, dancing, watching TV, taking or carrying human pictures in their pockets, playing cards, and not putting a turban on their heads for adults, was strictly prohibited.

Mullah Jabar raided many homes in the city of Kandahar, and confiscated TVs, radios, video players and such, and hung them on top of telephone pillars on the roads with a note reading: "Anyone who plays videotapes or watches TVs will be hung like this." His people would beat women who were wearing high heels. People were required to block the windows of their houses so women could not see outside.

"I would have extended the rule of the true Islam to other countries of the world had Taliban been ruling there." Mullah Jabar said answering a question by a Pakistani journalist.

"Don't you think that the people are feeling demoralized and disheartened under Taliban?" the journalist asked.

"If the people are the children of animals, yes they will be feeling demoralized and disheartened, but if they are the children of humans they will not." Mullah Jabar answered irritably.

"But you have taken away their freedoms."

"I told you, people are like animals, if you leave them alone they will smash everything under their feet."

"I have heard some people say that they feel like their country is now like a prison, and everyone is living in a prison."

"Only the children of animals will think so. I want to see anyone talking like that, and show them what prison means," answered Mullah furiously, his eyeballs protruding.

###

In late December 2001, Mullah Jabar was caught by surprise by a deafening explosion over the roof of his office, located in *Velayat*, the building of Kandahar governor. A US fighter jet roared like thunder in the sky and dropped a bomb on the building. He was lost in the rubble created by the bomb, and his left leg was severely injured. He crawled down to the basement, stayed there for a couple of hours until the bombing stopped. Then he was taken by ambulance to the Kandahar Civil Hospital for treatment, but after a quick stop, he ordered his subordinates to take him to Pakistan via a clandestine route.

Mullah had lost his left leg in the bombing and was given an artificial leg in a hospital in Quetta. After treatment, he stayed in Quetta under the protection of the ISI.

CHAPTER 4

THE NEW ERA

History repeated itself in Afghanistan. This formidable nation was invaded again by a world superpower. But unlike in the past, when it was invaded by other empires and superpowers such as Alexander the Great, Genghis Khan, The Mughal Empire, The Persian Empire, The British Empire, the Sikh Empire and the Soviet Empire, this time it was taken by the richest country in the human history, by the champion of democracy. In late 2001, the United States of America invaded Afghanistan under the pretext of defeating Al-Qaeda, for attacking the United States on 9/11/2001.

American invasion brought into the country a mood of democracy as well as the sense of rebuilding. But most importantly, it poured hundreds of billions of dollars into the country, from which benefited more than anyone else, individuals like Murad Khan, Shear Zaman and Mullah Jabar.

Murad Khan was now enjoying the chairmanship of the provincial council of Faryab, having two government paid bodyguards, the luxury of owning a palace in Kabul and the authority of commanding an over 500 armed private militia force, and in the meantime, earning countless money from his drug operation.

The day he convened his family meeting in his Taimany house, and after he lectured the meeting about his moral values, he ordered his older son, the chief of a police station in Kabul, to punish his renegade stepbrother, Samim, for trying to get married with Shear Zaman's daughter.

"Son, take this donkey to Andkhoy handcuffed and hand over him to my militia commander to hold him until I arrive back there. But you come back soon; I need you here."

Before returning to Andkhoy, Murad threw an impressive dinner party to which he invited army and police generals, parliamentarians, high-ranking governmental officials, Jihadi commanders and some reputable merchants.

"My dear brothers, generals, government leaders, Jihadi commanders, representatives of the people of Afghanistan and dignitaries," Murad addressed his guests after the huge dinner was served. "Your brother, Haji Murad, is wishing, as always, to serve his beloved country. So if you want to serve your country, you need to be someone in a higher position, if you are just a street person you cannot do anything for your country, so this time my wish is to serve my country as a member of the Afghan parliament. I really wish to be in the parliament one day, and I am asking you, my brothers, what do you think about this?"

"If a Jihadi commander doesn't deserve to be in the parliament, then who does?" shouted a former Jihadi commander.

"I will support you, Haji Murad Khan, you are my friend."

"Go for it; I will be with you Khan Sahib."

"You can do it, Haji Sahib; you have the money and the people behind you!" Complemented his guests one after the other.

Shear Zaman Tufan, as clever as he was in the past, was now running a lucrative busyness of construction in Kabul. When he returned from Moscow in 2002, he built a luxurious two-story house for himself in the Taimany area. He, in the meantime, established contacts both with the Afghan government authorities as well as with some Americans who were involved in the business of construction as he had realized that construction was going to be a much lucrative business. He got a license for forming a contraction company. He made contracts with domestic and foreign architectures and engineers and started signing construction contracts with the government and the US authorities.

Soon, Shear Zaman got the reputation of a successful contractor among the foreigners, especially American businessmen, who were desperate to find a native contractor to deal with when it came to building roads, buildings, and other constructions. There were tens of billions of US dollars available to be spent in the field. Within a year or two, he made more friends in the high governmental circles as well as within the NATO forces stationed in the country. As a former politician, he would sometimes, during private parties, lecture parliamentarians and government officials and even his American partners about the nuts and bolts of the Afghan politics and culture.

"You should be working for the government or be government leader because you are a seasoned politician," friends would tell Shear Zaman.

"Thank you, but I am so busy and happy with my business because here I am also serving the people of Afghanistan," He would reply, concealing, for the time being, his ambition for becoming a member of the Afghan parliament. He knew if he became a member of the parliament, he would have the opportunity to influence the government to sign more and more construction contracts with him, and in the meantime, achieve parliamentary immunity from being tried in the future for his criminal past.

Being proud of his performance as a madrassa teacher to have trained many suicidal Taliban, and being extremely jealous of Murad and Shear Zaman, Mullah Jabar could not forget the luxurious life he once had in Kabul. At that time he was staying in a furnished governmental guesthouse with a big screen TV set. He was provided with delicious foods three times a day along with every kind of fruits and juices. He particularly remembered the young man who would cook his food and a lady who would clean his room and make his bed every day. "That was like a heaven on the face of the earth," He would say to himself.

Now since there was once again the talk of making peace with the Taliban and other enemies, and many concessions being offered to them by the Afghan government and by NATO, he got the hope to intrude in the peace process. He closely followed the news and the rumors regarding some of the previous leaders of the Taliban movement coming to the side of the government or starting negotiations with it. A new organization by the name of National Peace Association of

Afghanistan was formed of high-ranking politicians, religious leaders, and tribal leaders.

This organization was particularly assigned with the task of bringing Taliban into the peace process; it would repeatedly issue calls to the Taliban to join them for bringing peace. The members of the organization would try to make personal contacts with Taliban as they were even called "Our Angry Brothers" by the president of the country.

"I am no less qualified than any other Taliban leaders to join the government," Mullah Jabar said to himself. He knew that he would not be easily accepted in the peace process as long as he was teaching the suicidal attackers; therefore, he reported to his superior that he was sick and his artificial leg was causing him severe pain when teaching. He was happy when he was replaced for the job by a young Talib, one of his former students. He went home in his village, kept a low profile, waiting for an opportunity to present itself. As a former drug tsar, he got, in the meantime, deeply involved in the drug business; he made deals with other drug dealers in Helman province, known as the major poppy growing place in the country. He remained associated with the Taliban as far as the drug business but politically tried to distance himself from the leadership of Taliban by making comments opposing its policies about killing civilians and burning school. He knew his comments were reaching the government authorities and the leadership of the National Peace Association. He maintained his ties with the Inter-Services Intelligence of Pakistan as well, just in case. The organization would also contact him time to time and provide him with advice how to infiltrate once again in the government body.

"Prepare yourself for a trip to Islamabad, for a meeting with important Pakistani authorities," this message was delivered to him by a personal messenger around three months after he left his teaching job.

"I am ready anytime you want me to, God willing," Mullah replied.

Two days later, he was picked up by a Hummer from his house, and driven all the way to Islamabad, where he was housed in an elegantly furnished guesthouse.

"Mullah Sahib, you are my favorite person among the Taliban leaders. I want you to play important role in Afghanistan's future," An ISI officer dressed in civilian clothes told him.

"God bless you and your country. I am the servant of Islam, I will do anything that's good for Muslims here or there," said Mullah Jabar, combing his long gray beard with the fingers of his right hand.

"I know, Mullah Sahib, you are a good Muslim. We wish to see you one day sitting in the Afghan parliament in Kabul."

Mullah combed his beard once again, as well as his mustache with the fingers of his right hand, trying to conceal his smile caused by the excitement of this idea. "God willing," Mullah echoed.

"You will be our guest here for a few weeks, and our people will be meeting with you every day, so you will not be bored."

"God willing."

Mullah was kept in the guesthouse for a month, visited by the ISI officers, training him for the future of Afghan politics.

As the three enemies were preparing for the same highly reputable political future for themselves, a wave of massive protests was getting momentum in Kabul and other major cities demanding justice for the victims of past crimes and atrocities. University students, intellectuals, the human rights advocates, civil rights communities, and countless Afghan individuals who had lost their family members, their houses, businesses as well as those who were physically or mentally incapacitated due to the crimes and atrocities, committed by political parties and individuals during the last two and a half decades,were demonstrating on the streets every day.

"Murderers, criminals, genocide perpetrators, human rights violators, national thieves and plunderers and drug dealers are walking free, they are still controlling the lives of the people of Afghanistan, we want them to be tried, and the justice is served." This was the slogan chanted by hundreds of thousands of demonstrators. The free media was also greatly echoing this demand over the TV stations, radios, and newspapers. The movement of justice attracted tremendous support from the world community as well. The then government was under tremendous pressure nationally and internationally to launch a legal campaign to bring justice to the country.

Murad, Shear Zaman, and Jabar were attentively watching the movement of demanding justice. Each one of them was anxiously following the events as they remembered their own acts of torture, killing and destroying lives. They were desperate and in need of help. They were seeking advice from their foreign friends.

"The only way to silence this noise and to rescue yourself from trouble in the future would be to become a member of the parliament where you can pass a law of general amnesty. This way you will be immune from any kind of legal trouble, and there will be no chance for the present or the future government to bother you," This was more or less the same advice given to each one of them by their foreign advisors.

From now on, the three could not wait to see themselves in the seats of the Afghan parliament. They would try extremely hard to campaign for themselves, and in the meantime, try to educate themselves about the principles of politics through following domestic, regional and international events. They would ask questions their foreign friends and advisers and have discussions with them in order to familiarize themselves with the basics of foreign politics.

The three were among the first group of the parliamentary hopefuls whose names were placed on the list of the candidates as soon as the process of registration started.

Murad was back and forth between Faryab and Kabul but mostly campaigning in Faryab. He had appointed the commander of his militia force as his campaign manager, who was known for his ruthlessness and toughness when it came to defending Murad Khan. The militia commander had received some education in Iran, and maintained a close relationship with his Iranian friends and enjoying their advice in leading Murad's parliamentary campaign.

"Son, don't worry about the money, you can spend as much as you want. Do everything in your power to send your big brother to the parliament," Murad told his campaign manager.

Shear Zaman realized that he needed to establish a reputation among the residents of his home province of Ghazni. He would frequently travel to the province and attend parties, political gatherings as well as Friday prayers in the mosques. In anticipation of the election, he had spent millions of Afghanis in rebuilding and decorating some historic and cultural sites in the province. Advised by his smart Russian advisor, he also spent a generous amount of money to feed the poor, and distributed to them important food items such as cooking oil, flour, and sugar.

Jabar was blessed with extraordinary support from his Pakistani friends. Months before the election, he was brought to his home province of Kandahar. He quickly infiltrated in the religious community by preaching the "Islamic Fraternity among all Muslims." He would travel from district to district, from village to village and from mosque to mosque to do the *Khairat-ul-Jomaa,* the Friday Charity. After the Friday prayer in a mosque, he would deliver a brief speech to the attendees and then invite them to take home alms, which he would announce that he was giving away in the name of Allah. The one serving size of raw beef, already prepared by Jabar's people in front of the mosque, would be given to each of the men on their way home. The recipients, mostly poor people, who had not been able to buy meat for their families even once a month, would greatly appreciate the charity and some would even bend and kiss Mullah Jabar's hands at the receipt of the fresh meat.

As the time of the election was approaching, the three candidates intensified their campaign efforts. Their large colorful portraits were posted on the big boards and the walls of the buildings in their respective cities. Their campaign fliers were flying everywhere on the streets; young children were advertising their pictures, their names and slogans printed in the local and national newspapers. Murad's motto was: ISLAM, JIHAD, and HOMELAND. Shear Zaman's slogan was printed as ISLAM, PROGRESS, and HOMELAND. Mullah Jabar's poster was decorated with the slogan of ISLAM, SHARIA, and HOMELAND.

Many influential circles in the Afghan government, and some of the neighboring countries such as Pakistan, Iran, Russia, as well as NATO countries, especially the United States, were all hoping to get their favorite persons into the highest legislative body. Thus, each one of the three, Murad, Shear Zaman and Mullah Jabar got friends and supporters both among domestic politicians as well as among foreigners.

Murad was counting on his old friends in Iran and was following their instructions. Shear Zaman maintained his good relationship with Russians and listened to them in every step of the way. And Jabar had received assurances and help from his Pakistani friends and was doing whatever they would ask him to do.

The day, the election of 2005 was over, none of the three could sleep almost the whole night; they all separated themselves from their friends and campaign teams early in the night, pretending sleeplessness and tiredness of the campaign period, wishing to get alone with their thoughts and dreams. Murad tried to console his mix feelings of anxiety and enthusiasm by smoking a *cigretty-* a home-made hashish cigar in the balcony of his Taimany house. Besides, he emptied a whole pack of American L&M cigarettes by the time of Morning Prayer. Shear Zaman spent the night in the living room of his house by drinking Stolichnaya vodka and smoking the same brand of cigarettes as Murad did. Jabar, residing in a glorious house in the New City in Kandahar, smoked a heavy hashish hookah after his night prayer in the hope that it would put him to sleep comfortably. But he woke up at midnight, tossed and turned in his bed until morning.

After the results were announced a week after the election, the three celebrated their victory by throwing extravagant dinner parties in their residences, inviting among others many dignitaries, tens of their fellow parliamentarians– excluding the other two. In the meantime, they prepared themselves for facing each other and sitting in the same chamber with each other.

They got enthusiastically involved in doing the "business of the people." They would meet with cabinet members claiming to promote the interest of their respective constituencies. Sometimes they would meet with the president and try every possible occasion to get their names mentioned in the news. They were, in the meantime, competing with each other in making friends and in making groups with other parliament members. But they would not talk to each other; they would even make antagonistic statements against each other on the floor of the House of Representatives.

Murad Khan once addressing the parliament and discussing a civil rights bill said, "This is a shame for this house of the nation that here we have among us the communists, terrorists and national traitors who are responsible for the killing of hundreds of thousands of our innocent people."

In his turn, speaking about the same issue, Shear Zaman, turning to Murad and Jabar, stated: "This place, this house of the nation, would have been a better and a more effective national body had historic murderers, plunderers, and drug dealers not been sitting here amongst us."

When the floor was turned over to Jabar, he also targeted the other two by stating that, "We all are Muslims, we all are the servants of the people, but unfortunately we have some infidels, some national traitors, and foreign agents, who are in the service of other countries, present here among us."

During the year 2007, huge demonstrations were launched in front of the building of the House of Representatives. Tens of thousands of participants chanted the slogan of "Death to the national traitors, murderers, infidels, foreign agents and drug dealers! This is not the house of nation. This is a safe haven for the historic enemies of the people of Afghanistan. We want justice; we want them to be put on trial!" Soon, the movement spread over to the bigger cities, and newly formed civil rights organizations actively voiced the cause of the justice. During the demonstrations, there were incidences of attacking luxury cars carrying Murad, Shear Zaman and Jabar with eggs and stones. The government was forced to allocate a two person armed security guard and an armored vehicle to each of the parliament members for their protection.

But nothing would silence the demand for justice which was loudly voiced all over the country. A handful of parliament members who had not been accused of shedding blood or committing national treason, also joined the forces outside the parliament, intensifying the demand that justice should be served and the perpetrators are put on trial as soon as possible.

CHAPTER 5

MR. CALLAHAN

Extremely desperate for help, each one of the three men discussed the situation with their foreign advisors and sought various possible ways to rescue themselves from the trial as they realized that there existed sufficient documents and witnesses to testify against them if they were put on trial. They were advised to contact their friends inside the parliament and try to form an alliance in the parliament and pass a law of general amnesty. This idea appealed more than ever before to the three as well as to many others in the parliament.

But there existed a huge problem in achieving this goal. The three powerful men, Haji Murad, Shear Zaman and Mullah Jabar, would not get along, and would not even talk to each other. Everyone in the House of Representatives knew that they were the bloodthirsty enemy of the other two. There was no way for them to get along with each other, even each one was plotting against the others.

Murad's "Green Eyed" friend, who used to provide advice to him in the times of the Jihad, was watching the situation closely. The American politician, who wished to be called Mr. Callahan, had just returned to Kabul with a new mission. He would introduce himself to everyone as a businessman and tried to be seen making business contracts with the defense ministry of Afghanistan as well as with the NATO forces. His intelligence expertise gave him the ability to be on top of the situation. If he had knowledge of Murad from the past, he was likewise very well aware of where Shear Zaman and Jabar came from, what their pasts were and what ambitions they had. He knew very will that all three of them were powerful individuals. Besides being a millionaire, Murad Khan had a thousand armed militiamen behind him. Also, Shear Zaman had returned from Moscow with millions of dollars and had strong connections with the governmental authorities as well as with large construction companies. Mullah Jabar was credited with having an influence on many Taliban groups who might be beneficial for future deals.

Mr. Callahan, a tall, heavy stature, 65 years old Texan man with gray hair, and green eyes had been involved in the South Asian and Middle East politics for decades. He had spent the whole decade of the 1980s in Pakistan and Afghanistan. Before that, he spent eight years in Iran from 1970 until the king of Iran was deposed. He had met with Murad and many other jihadi commanders in the time of the jihad and gave them advice. He played an important role in delivering the US financial aid to the Mujahedeen.

When Mr. Callahan concluded that the time was ripe for him to enter the political game; he contacted Murad with a congratulatory message followed by a request for one on one meeting. Murad desperately accepted the meeting hoping to get the right advice and help from him.

"As I anticipated in the past, you are now an important person in the political scene of Afghanistan. I wish you further success," said Mr. Callahan in fluent Farsi.

"Thank you, Mr. Callahan. You came back at the right time; I need your advice regarding the current situation. I am sure you know that currently, we have problems with that street noise launched by some ill-trained kids, who are being instigated against me and some other members of the parliament by foreign agents."

"I know, Khan Sahib, but what do you think should be done about it?" Mr. Callahan asked.

"I don't know; some people say that there should be a law of amnesty in place to silence these noises forever."

"Maybe they are right. You, the representatives of the people should do exactly that. You and other members of the parliament should get together and pass such a law."

"You know, Mr. Callahan, in this parliament we have people like Shear Zaman and Jabar who are my enemies, and they are criminals, how can I be together with them?"

"Yes, you can. And you should forget about the past. Now they also need you, and you need them, all of you need each other for the good of the people. If you are fighting among yourselves, none of you will be able to serve your people and your country."

"My conscience would not permit me to talk to them Mr. Callahan, especially to Shear Zaman. I very much hate him." Murad Khan said after a relatively longer silence. "And Jabar too, you might not be aware that he recently tried to kill me by a suicidal attack."

"I know, Khan Sahib, I know. But you should realize that they might have the same feelings toward you. I am aware of the fact that you guys can not initiate a contact with each other, I can help bring you together if you permit me."

"If you think we need each other for the good of the people and the country, then you are permitted to do whatever you want, but I swear to God I will never forgive Shear Zaman for killing my brother."

"I know Khan Sahib, I respect your feelings, but the good of the people and the country is bigger than your feelings, you need to make sacrifices."

Mr. Callahan got what he needed from Murad. Murad approved his Green Eyed Friend's plan to bring peace among the three enemies.

After two weeks of shuttle diplomacy, Mr. Callahan's expertise in the field also helped him achieve Shear Zaman's and Mullah Jabar's approval.

"You know, you are one of those afghans that I have always thought of a wise and respected man who can step over his selfishness and make a sacrifice for the good of others. No doubt, whenever you make a sacrifice for the good of others, others will do the same for you and you will eventually benefit from you own sacrifice. I am sure you realize that there will be many occasions when you have others on your side, you will be able to pass laws like this one and also pass contracts worthy of huge amounts of money, you, yourself will benefit greatly." This was the lecture that Mr. Callahan repeatedly gave to each of the three in his one on one meetings with them. He would meet with them sometimes in the US embassy in Kabul, giving them the impression that he had the backing of his government as well.

By the time a draft Law of Amnesty was presented to the parliament, in which he played a role, Mr. Callahan's efforts succeeded in at least stopping the three from talking bad against each other; they also convinced their friends and followers to cooperate with the others in passing the law. Consequently, in 2007, they joined forces and campaigned together to get the law of General Amnesty passed. Despite the widespread protests, the law was published in the official gazette of the country and became the law of the land in 2009. The law provided a safe haven for the three and other criminals. In Article one it said: "This law is adopted for the purpose of strengthening the reconciliation and national stability, ensuring the supreme interests of the country, ending rivalries and building confidence among the belligerent parties, based on their immunity in the case of adherence to the Constitution."

"All political factions and hostile parties who were involved in a way or another in hostilities before establishing of the Interim Administration shall be included in the reconciliation and general amnesty program for the purpose of reconciliation among different segments of society, strengthening of peace and stability and starting of new life in the contemporary political history of Afghanistan, and enjoy all their legal rights and shall not be legally and judicially prosecuted."

Mr. Callahan could not conceal his excitement on the occasion of the passage of this law when he saw his friends were satisfied with what he had suggested for their good. Not wasting time, he planned the second phase of bringing reconciliation among the three by inviting them to a dinner at the Serena Hotel restaurant, the most luxurious and expensive place in Kabul. But before inviting them to the dinner, he met with and congratulated them one on one. He stressed the importance of this historic victory and told them that it was worth celebrating in a big way. Murad was hesitant at having the dinner at the same table with Shear Zaman and Jabar. The latter two were also uneasy to accept this idea. But referring to the contents of the first article of the law during his discussions with them, Mr. Callahan was able to convince each one of them that they should begin the process of achieving the national reconciliation from themselves.

Jabar was the first to arrive at the restaurant. He turned his head away when Shear Zaman joined him at the dinner table. Murad arrived thirty minutes late; he shook hand with Mr. Callahan but didn't even look at the other two.

"Dear friends and distinguished members of the Afghan parliament," Mr. Callahan addressed his guests. "Today we are here to celebrate the historic victory of the Afghan people in passing a law which will bring peace and unity among the different factions of the society. I firmly believe that the passage of this law will bring progress and prosperity to the nation. This historic achievement is particularly important to you distinguished members of the parliament as you will be having peace of mind when doing the business of your people."

Each one of the three thanked Mr. Callahan for his advice and efforts in this regard, and for inviting them to the dinner. The dinner party ended without Murad, Shear Zaman, and Jabar even talking a word to each other.

Mr. Callahan saw this gathering as a success and started thinking about the next step. Two days later, he met again with all three of them one on one. This time he discussed with them the issue of a contract regarding providing petroleum to the Ministry of Defense of Afghanistan.

"If this contract is passed by the parliament, your country will benefit economically, and it would bring thousands of jobs in the area of the transportation workforce," Mr. Callahan explained individually to Murad, Shear Zaman, and Jabar. "I understand that without your help this contract cannot be approved. I further understand that you have a lot of friends in the defense ministry, and can influence the leadership there to sign the contract with me. You can also make contacts with your fellow representatives to vote for the contract."

Before getting the contract signed with him, Mr. Callahan said, "I know that nowadays everything costs money. Campaigning for an important matter such as this and bringing more parliament members to your side requires hundreds of thousands of dollars, which is a normal thing and I am ready to spend it. I believe if this contract is given to me your efforts will surely be rewarded."

His three friends got the message.

"How much is he going to pay me? He knows that I am stronger than the other two and can bring more representatives and some senators to the floor of the parliament to vote for the contract," Murad asked himself.

In his next joint meeting with the three, Mr. Callahan stressed that money will do it. He gazed at everyone's face to see how they react to the incentive.

"I can utilize the influence of my Pakistani friends over some of the parliament members to rally support for the passing of the contract. Now I have many friends in the Senate too, but as you said, nowadays everything costs money. Maybe I will need to spend at least fifty thousand dollars," Mullah Jabar mentioned passionately

"I totally agree with you Mullah Sahib," Mr. Callahan said. "But I think nowadays the cost of living has gone up very much, life is expensive. Therefore, I believe more than the amount you mentioned will be needed, but you don't worry about the money, my pocket is open for you, you can spend as much as needed."

All three of them nodded with a smile.

It was one month later that Callahan's contract with Defense Ministry was granted according to his wishes. His three friends received their share of the reward. Mr. Callahan, envisioning more future financial and political deals in the country, sought further unity and even friendship among his three friends, and planned to bring a formal alliance among them. Therefore, on the occasion of the approval of the contract, he invited them to a picnic party in the Spozhmay Restaurant in Qargha, outside of Kabul city. None of the three had ever been to this exotic place. Only dignitaries and rich people from the capital used to picnic in the Qargha restaurant and resort located by the clear water dam surrounded by mountains. All got excited. The food from the restaurant was astonishing; the moon was shining in the clear blue sky. Mr. Callahan was appreciating the weather and the atmosphere. He was telling stories from America and making jokes that made his companions laugh. By the time *baghlawa* and *fereny* were served with coffee and green tea, the three started looking at each other with a smile on their lips and even nodding to each other while talking or listening to their Green Eyed friend. They were enjoying the party, feeling confident of a bright and lucrative future for their alliance.